Vengeance at Tyburn Ridge

Something caused Robert Angelo to return to Tyburn Ridge – the town where he once was a lawman – and someone killed him when he arrived there. Now his son, Casey, is determined to seek vengeance for his father's murder. But it will not prove to be an easy mission.

Bullied as a child in Tyburn Ridge, Casey finds his old enemies are still in town – and more eager than ever to humiliate and hurt him. Whilst searching for the truth, Casey is framed for the murder of a saloon girl.

Now he must turn his tormentors' weaknesses against them and discover the identity of the killers, if vengeance is to be served.

Vengeance at Tyburn Ridge

Derek Rutherford

A Black Horse Western

ROBERT HALE · LONDON

© Derek Rutherford 2005
First published in Great Britain 2005

ISBN 0 7090 7666 5

Robert Hale Limited
Clerkenwell House
Clerkenwell Green
London EC1R 0HT

Typeset by
Derek Doyle & Associates, Liverpool.
Printed and bound in Great Britain by
Antony Rowe Limited, Wiltshire

CHAPTER ONE

They were waiting for Casey Angelo on the platform. The four of them standing there just the way they had been ten years earlier when Casey's father had taken his family East. They had been laughing then, and they were laughing now. Casey could almost read their minds: *It's good to have you back, Yellow. We've missed all that fun we used to have.*

Casey stepped down from the train and stared at them. There stood Hudson Ranier, the tallest of the four. He had long black hair, a thin hawklike nose, mean beady eyes and a hot temper. He'd grown a little, but other than that and the fact his hair was longer he looked pretty much the way he had when he was younger. Next to him Campbell James, with his red hair bearding his face now. He'd broadened out, his shoulders were wider and his chest deeper than Casey remembered. Milton Craig was the smallest. But ever since Casey had known him Milton had possessed a mean streak deep enough to compensate for his lack of inches. Milton's face had always reminded Casey of a rat. His skin was pock-marked and Casey remembered him once cutting another boy's cheeks with a knife just because the boy had laughed at Milton's complexion. Lastly at the far left, John Stark, standing very still and upright: the only one of the four who had ever appeared to consider the consequences of what they were doing. The fact that he always carried on regardless seemed to Casey to make him the most dangerous of all.

'We heard you were coming home, Yellow,' Hudson said, looking even taller with the wide expanse of cold sky and the mountains behind him. 'Figured we'd be here to meet you. Make you welcome, like.'

Casey nodded slowly, giving nothing away, not scared, but at the same time aware that the impression of fear might be worth giving. It might keep them off guard.

'Cat got your tongue?' Milton said, and giggled.

'It's good to see you again, Casey,' John Stark said, and nodded.

'His name's Yellow,' Milton said. 'Always was. Always will be.'

They had tied a noose around Casey's neck one time, thrown and tied the loose end over a cottonwood down by Jagged Creek, and at gunpoint had forced him to climb on to Hudson's pony. Then they had threatened to stampede the pony by firing the gun right by its ear. Casey had never been so scared in his entire life. The pony had stood there grazing on the lush grass oblivious to the fact that just a few meandering steps forward and Casey would have been swinging in the breeze like an outlaw with no luck left. They told him later that it had been a false knot. That even if the pony had bolted Casey would have just wound up in a heap on the floor. Casey hadn't believed them then, and now, seeing them standing with their hats cocked forwards, their coats open despite the freezing temperature and the snow that lay on the ground, and their guns hanging off their hips, he had no reason to change his mind. They had always wanted to be dangerous and feared. And maybe if a man believes something long and hard enough then it becomes real.

They were five years older than Casey. And whilst such a gap makes a big difference when you're ten and your tormentors are fifteen, it doesn't mean so much ten years later.

'Sorry to hear about your pa,' Campbell said, stifling his grin. 'Commiserations and all that.'

At last Casey spoke. 'I'm sorry, too.'

It was why he was back in Tyburn Ridge. He'd come to collect his father. Robert Angelo was lying in a sealed coffin in the undertaker's yard.

Murdered.

The undertaker's name was Hap Smith. He was a bald fellow with round spectacles that gave him an air of intelligence and who always dressed in black. When Casey and the others had been kids they'd nicknamed him Happy. It was Hap who had sent the telegram to Casey and his mother in Omaha.

'I don't know as I'd have bothered if it was anyone else,' he said. 'But Robert was a fine man. It was the least I could do.'

'I'm grateful to you.'

He shook his head. 'No, it's us who should be grateful. We could do with a lawman like Robert round these parts again.'

'What's up? Have things changed?'

The walk from the station into town had seemed peaceful enough. Though Hudson and his gang had trailed Casey like a pack of hopeful coyotes, keeping their distance and laughing all the way, their heels crunching on the frozen ground and their mocking voices reminding Casey of all the humiliating things they'd done to him before his father had taken his family away from Tyburn Ridge. Casey had ignored them, raised his collar against the cruel wind and headed as quickly as he could – given the ice under-foot – for the shelter of town. It was February and although the sky was cloudless all the way to the mountains the air was cold enough to freeze eyebrows and crack lips. The coyotes gave up as soon as he passed Sloppy's Saloon and he was alone by the time he reached Hap's.

The town *had* changed a lot since Casey had last been

there. The station was the most obvious addition. The rail-road had passed about a mile north of Tyburn Ridge and now the town was slowly reaching out towards it. Adobes, whitewashed with *jaspe* dotted the surrounding landscape and were almost invisible against the drifting snow, and the town itself had expanded in all directions. On his way to Hap's he passed numerous false-fronted businesses including two saloons, of which Sloppy's was the first. Looking further towards the centre of town, beyond the well, he could see a church that hadn't been there ten years back.

'Maybe I shouldn't moan,' Hap said now. 'Business has rarely been so good.'

'And who's doing all this killing?'

'No one in particular. There's just a general feeling of . . . lawlessness.'

'And my father?' Casey asked. 'Who killed him?'

He had travelled 300 miles, not just to bring his father's body home, but to ask that very question.

Hap shook his head. 'Nobody knows.'

It wasn't the answer Casey had wanted.

'Nobody?'

'Let me pour you a drink,' Hap said. 'You look freezing. Sit down and I'll tell you what little I know.'

'Can I see him first?'

Hap sighed. The look in Casey's eyes told him there was little point in arguing.

'You're lucky it's winter. If this was August I'd have buried him the day they brought him in.'

Lucky was the last thing Casey felt: his father rode out one day and a few days later a telegram arrived from Tyburn Ridge saying his body is at the undertaker's and would someone care to come and collect it?

Hap led him out into the yard where several empty pine coffins were laid upon each other in a precarious looking pile. Their lids were stacked up next to a black four-wheeled wagon. It looked as if Hap was well prepared for the next round of unlawfulness.

Against the building itself there was a tarpaulin covering another coffin. This one had its lid screwed down. Hap started to pull the tarp back. It crackled where it had frozen. Casey felt water welling in his eyes. Before the water could become tears it froze on his eyelids and he had to brush the tiny icicles away.

His father had been his one and only hero. His teacher, too. A fearless lawman; a man with a sense of right and wrong as clear as day and night; a man who commanded respect and love in equal measures. He had been tall and had walked straight. He had been the most handsome man Casey had ever seen. The strongest, too. And the gentlest. He had never shot a man without first giving that man the opportunity to walk himself straight into the cell and throw himself on the mercy of a circuit judge. Some had done just that. Some had elected to stand and fight. And die.

'Maybe I should have a look first,' Hap said. 'On my own, you know. Just to make sure that . . .'

'It's OK, Hap,' Casey said. 'Just open the coffin.'

It seemed an eternity before Hap had undone all of the screws. Slowly, he eased the lid off the coffin and stepped away. Casey swallowed and looked down at his father.

Casey had heard it said that some people didn't recognize their own kin in death, that once the blood had stopped pulsing and the muscles relaxed and the cheeks and eyes sank into the skull that someone you once saw every day can look like a stranger. He wasn't sure he believed such things. Maybe it was just wishful thinking on the part of people asked to identify a loved one and hoping against hope that it wasn't going to be their kin. *His* father looked, in death, just as he looked in life. Paler and a little thinner maybe. But his chiselled features and thick hair and strong bones were instantly recognizable.

'Where did they—'

'In the chest,' Hap said. 'Twice.' He stepped forwards and gently pulled Robert Angelo's coat open. Like the tarp, it crackled as he moved it. Beneath the coat Robert Angelo had been wearing a suit and his favourite yellow shirt that now had a small hole and a large stain over the heart. 'The second shot was further across,' Hap said, opening up the other side of the jacket. 'I'd say that they were fired in quick succession. The first went right through the heart and maybe spun him round a little. The second could only have been a moment later.'

Casey wiped more icicles from his eyes. The last time they'd spoken his father had been saddling up a grey mare with the intention of heading out towards Fort Kearney, or at least the remains of the fort – the Cheyenne had burned it down twelve years before. Word was there were two dozen fine horses – maybe more – that he could have for a good price. That was the story he'd told Casey the night before he'd left anyway. But what was he doing taking his only suit and his favourite shirt on a horse drive?

'Look after your ma,' his father had said that morning. His mother had been standing in the doorway and his father had looked at her for a long time. They had both been smiling deep in their eyes. Then his father had tipped his hat, turned that grey mare on a penny, and had ridden into the cold sun. He'd done the same thing a hundred times since the family had moved East.

Casey swallowed again and tried to compose himself.

'His gun?' he asked.

'It's locked away in my office,' Hap said. 'I didn't know whether you'd want it buried with him or not.'

Casey nodded, not knowing yet either.

'Had it been fired?'

'No. Leastways not unless someone cleaned it and loaded it again.'

Casey tried to picture the scene. His father wouldn't have been taken in a gunfight. Not so easily. Not without loosing off at least one shot. So he'd been ambushed. Walked right into it.

'You think they were rifle bullets that killed him?' Casey asked.

'I'm not sure,' Hap said. Then he voiced Casey's own thoughts almost to the syllable: 'But if I know Robert then I'd guess so. I don't think he'd have been taken so easily in a fair fight.'

Casey stood there a while longer. It didn't seem right that he ask for his father to be covered up again. Once that coffin lid was closed again that would be Robert Angelo gone for ever. Hap came to his rescue.

'Come on, son,' he said. 'Let's pour you that drink.'

Back in the office, a glass of whiskey clenched in one trembling hand, a cigarette in the other, Casey asked Hap if there had been anything in his father's pockets. He still didn't know why Robert had been back here in Tyburn Ridge.

'Nothing,' Hap said.

'Nothing? Not even money?'

'Nothing.'

'Then it could have been a straight robbery?'

'Casey, your father was a good man. A good *law*man. He put a lot of people in jail and more than a few hung because of him. He made a lot of friends but just as many enemies. This wasn't a straight robbery.'

Casey downed the rest of his whisky in one hit. 'I'm going to find out, Hap. I swear I shan't rest until I've found out who killed him.'

'And then what?'

Casey looked into Hap's eyes, seeing his own reflection in the man's spectacles. 'Then I'll do the right thing,' he said.

CHAPTER TWO

Hap recommended that Casey stay at Mrs Martha Slade's boarding house, though he did also warn Casey that Martha liked to talk a lot. There was a rumour that Mrs Slade's husband had lit out for Salt Lake City several years back not just to find out if there was a better living to be made there but simply for some peace and quiet. Whether or not he found a fortune or just a blessed silence wasn't known – he'd never returned. That aside, Hap said, Martha's tariffs were fair, her rooms clean, and she'd feed you pretty well, too. She had arrived in town in the years since the Angelos had left and consequently Casey had never seen her before. He guessed she was in her forties. She had thick red hair that was pinned up on top of her head, a pretty face, and a full figure. The first thing she said after Casey had paid her his board was, 'Hot food, or a hot bath?' He plumped for the bath. The cold air had found its way deep into his bone marrow. By the time he had dried himself and dressed there was a plate of hot stew on the table.

'You came in on the train,' she said, leaning against the door watching him. He didn't know whether she was asking a question or making a statement.

'Yep.'

She nodded. 'Where are you from?'

He was from right here, from Tyburn Ridge. This was

12

his home town. But he figured she meant where did he come from on the train.

'Omaha.'

'Omaha. They say that's a mighty big city.'

'Yep. We've got the Union Pacific to thank for that.'

'They say the lights are something to behold.' It was dusk outside and Martha's kitchen was lit by just three oil-lamps.

'So they say, but we live outside of the city.'

'Oh. You're not with the railroad then?'

'We buy and sell horses.' As Casey spoke he felt that chill creeping back into his bones. *We* was no longer.

'You don't look very old.'

'I'm twenty.'

'And you're here to buy horses?'

'No,' he said, and paused. There was little point in being secretive. He'd need to talk to everyone he could. And maybe someone who was as inquisitive as Martha Slade would be the perfect person to start with. 'I'm here to collect my father.'

'He's been buying horses?'

'No. He's dead.'

She put a hand to her mouth. 'Oh. I'm sorry.'

'It's OK.'

'What happened?'

'That's what I'd like to know,' Casey said, and looked up from his stew. 'Someone shot him.'

Earlier Hap had told Casey how two ranch hands from Franklin Hicks's Double Z had found Robert Angelo's body about twenty minutes out of town to the west. A blizzard had been getting up and it was only by chance that Jake Bowers and Clifford Tanner had spotted him. They'd hoisted his father's body across the back of Jake's horse and had brought him into town. That was about all that was known. If Casey wanted to talk to them the Double Z

13

was about an hour away, though it was likely the boys would be in town come the weekend.

Now he asked Martha if she'd heard anything about it.

'Of course,' she said. 'It was the talk of the Ridge for a day.' She then went on to recount pretty much exactly what Hap had already told him. Except that at the end she added: 'They say there was a woman involved, too.'

'A woman?'

'Yes. A woman. Apparently . . .' She paused, looked across at him, and bit her lower lip. 'Maybe I shouldn't say.'

'Maybe you should. Apparently what?'

'Well it was that Suzie Cobb who said about it and she's as likely to have made it up as not.'

'Suzie Cobb?'

'She works at Sloppy's. Works upstairs, if you know what I mean.'

'And what did Suzie Cobb say?'

Martha shook her head. 'I'm sure she just made it up. She likes to make out that she knows something other folk don't.'

'Martha.' Casey could see that she was uncomfortable. And people rarely got uncomfortable over nothing.

She pulled a face as if she'd swallowed something unpleasant.

'She told me that the fellow got what he deserved, cheating on his wife like that.'

Casey felt blood warming his face. He dropped his spoon and clenched his fists, lowering them to below the level of the table so not as to scare Martha. But she must have noticed because she said quickly:

'I told you. It's make-believe. It's just what I heard.'

He breathed deeply and slowly. He could still recall the smile that his father and mother had exchanged on that last morning. They were very much in love. His father was no cheat. And he told Martha as much.

'Suzie Cobb's as mean as a rattlesnake,' she said. 'In a year or two she'll be all used up and she's already bitter about it.'

'What did she mean? You must have asked her.'

'She wouldn't let on. That's typical Suzie. Wants to let you know she knows something but won't tell you. Not all at once, anyway. She likes people to beg her.'

'Tell me again what she said.'

'Someone told her that he – your father – had been to see a woman. And it was the woman's husband that shot him.'

Dusk was turning to night outside. There were flurries of fresh snow against the window. Casey's bones were feeling cold again and the day's travelling and emotions had wearied him. But determination overrode everything. He stood up. The evening and night-time were when Suzie Cobb would be available.

'I think I'll go pay Suzie a visit,' he said. 'See if I can't beg a little.'

Casey left his Colt .45 buried deep in his roll at Martha's and headed to Sloppy's unarmed. It was his father's teaching. He'd told Casey that of all the men he had seen hang only a few had been truly bad. The rest were simply fools who had wandered around in the mistaken belief that the gun strapped to their hip made them invincible and right.

'Most of them were very vincible and usually wrong,' he had said. 'Those that didn't die in a gunfight usually hung soon after.'

The music inside Sloppy's didn't stop as he closed the door and shut out the icy wind and the snow, but it felt that way. All the conversation faltered and the piano player hit a few wrong notes as he glanced over his shoulder to see what the sudden hush was about. Casey paused

15

just inside the saloon. There was only one girl in the saloon. A redhead standing at the far end of the bar by the stove. She needed to be near the heat, the corset she was wearing left her arms and shoulders bare. It wasn't Suzie Cobb, though. Before he'd left Martha's she had given him a pretty good description of Suzie and this wasn't her. Casey brushed a little snow off his shoulders and made eye contact with as many of the men in the saloon as possible – the card-players, the fellows standing by the piano, the old-timers huddled round the stove even more interested in the warmth than the redhead, and last of all, Hudson and his pack, who were leaning up against the bar, grinning at him. As the shadows from the oil-lamps danced continuously Casey watched everyone, searching for a flicker of nervousness, a brief indication of guilt maybe. But there was nothing. What he did see in all of those eyes was recognition. No doubt Hudson and the boys had been enjoying holding court with Casey Angelo as their topic of conversation.

'Well looky here,' Hudson said, his voice slightly slurred. 'It's young Yellow, come to take his poor daddy home.'

'He won't find him in here,' Milton said, and laughed. 'Though it might be worth trying Happy's, Yellow.'

'I've been to Hap's already,' Casey said, and started towards the bar.

'How was he?' Hudson said.

'Hap was fine,' Casey said. He went to the left of Hudson's group, rested a boot on the rail and nodded at the barman.

'I'll get you that, Casey,' John Stark said. 'What'll it be?'

'His name's Yellow.'

'Shut up, Milton,' Stark said.

Casey looked at Stark. Of all of them he was the only one showing any respect or civility. But at the same time he

16

still exuded the greatest aura of danger. It was almost like he had grown up whilst the others were still acting like kids.

'Thanks, John,' Casey said. 'Whiskey'll do just fine.'

Stark ordered the whiskey along with a pitcher of beer to wash it down with.

'So you seen your daddy, then,' Hudson said.

'Yep.'

'It ain't nice, is it? I mean, having to look down on your own dead father.'

Casey waited for the barman to pour his whiskey and place it in front of him, then he lifted the glass and downed the drink in a single shot, savouring the warm explosion that filled his mouth, throat, and belly. He put the glass down on the bar lightly, not making a sound.

Casey turned towards Hudson. The man's eyes were bloodshot. His teeth were tobacco-stained, his skin dark with dirt. But his gaze was steady and challenging.

'There's a difference between cold blood and the due process of law,' Casey said.

'You saying my daddy deserved to hang?'

'I was too young to know, Hud. But that's exactly what a judge decided.'

He watched Hudson's eyes. It was easy to understand now what his father had meant about fools and guns. An exchange such as this, tough and touching on raw nerves, could easily lead to a gunfight. Casey could sense the tension building within Hudson. There seemed to be as much hate as there was alcohol inside him. Yet Casey understood the need for vengeance. The Peacemaker he had wrapped in his blanket back at Martha Slade's wasn't there just for company.

'But there wouldn't have been no judge needed if your father hadn't meddled in affairs that were nothing to do with him,' Hudson said.

17

Casey's eyes flicked down to Hudson's hands. They were steady on the bar but he noticed the man's jacket was pulled back clear of his gun.

'He wasn't meddling,' Casey said. 'He was doing his job.'

The way Casey understood it – and the understanding came only from various snippets of overheard conversation and hearsay because no one had ever sat down and told him the story straight – was that Hudson's father, Spencer Ranier, had shot dead a young man and his wife who had been passing through Tyburn Ridge. Spencer had sworn it was self-defence, that the man had come for him with a Bowie knife after Spencer had jokingly made mention that the Indians would love a girl as pretty as that one and maybe he'd best leave her behind with Spencer for safekeeping. The story could have held up, too, had they ever found a Bowie knife and had Spencer been able to give a good reason why he'd also shot the girl. Then there had been the witness. A fellow by the name of Blue McGinty, who left Tyburn Ridge after the trial, fearing for his own safety, had been riding out by the trail where it happened and said he had seen the man tied up to a tree – and sure enough there were rope burns on the man's wrists and they found the rope on the ground by the tree in question. McGinty hadn't known what was happening so he had cut the man loose and had only then heard the crying and moaning of a woman coming from the stranger's covered wagon. The untied man had rushed across to his wagon and that had been when Spencer had killed him and his wife.

'If your daddy was only doing his job why did he run like a scared dog afterwards,' Hudson said. 'Tell me that, Yellow.'

Now the piano player had stopped playing and had turned to watch them.

18

'He didn't run,' Casey said. He knew in his heart that his father would never run from anyone, but he had nothing to back the statement up with. It was still a mystery to him why they'd left Tyburn Ridge in such a hurry all those years ago.

'That's exactly what he did. Maybe that's where you get your yellow streak from, Casey.'

Casey took a slow deep breath. Perhaps he should have worn his gun, after all. He'd come to Tyburn Ridge to kill someone. Why not get the job done right away?

'Cat got your tongue?' Milton said.

'He turned my daddy over to the judge and was gone in a fortnight,' continued Hudson. 'And I'll tell you one more thing, Yellow.'

'What's that?'

'I danced a goddamn jig when I heard your daddy'd been shot dead.'

Casey clenched his fists. Another thing his father had told him: stay calm, don't fight with the blood roaring through your veins, that's what they want. It messes up your judgement and buries your instincts. Don't let their words hurt you. It's their fists and guns you have to be wary of. So fight on your own terms. Let them be the ones to get riled. Good words, but sometimes it was so hard to resist the rushing blood.

'What's the matter, Casey?' Hudson said. 'Don't like what you're hearing but too yellow to do anything about it?'

The mocking tone in Hudson's voice was almost too much to bear. Despite all of his father's warnings Casey tensed his muscles and prepared to launch himself at Hudson. Right then he wanted nothing more than to pound his fists against Hudson's bones, feel the man's teeth crack, and wipe the laughter from his face. He would have done it, too, but Hudson's saviour came in the shape of Suzie Cobb. Casey saw the girl at the top of the stairs, on the landing that ran along the back wall of the saloon, and recognized her from Martha's description. A man was just descending the stairs, tucking in his trousers and blushing slightly. At the bar Hudson was still grinning and snarling simultaneously, oblivious to the fact that Casey's attention was briefly diverted. Already Casey was thinking beyond a fight, breathing deeply, trying to control his fury and stay focused on doing what he'd come here to do – which was to talk to Suzie Cobb. He'd allowed himself to get riled. But it wasn't too late.

His eyes flicked back to Hudson. 'Forget it,' he said.

'What do you mean "forget it"?' Hudson had been ready for a fight. A man couldn't just back down.

'I guess you and I got a lot to talk about, Hud,' Casey said. 'Starting with an apology on your part. But right now there's someone I've got to see.'

'Huh?' Hudson sounded confused. The adrenaline and whiskey running through his veins were still anxious for release but suddenly his quarry was backing off.

'Yellow. Always was, always will be,' Milton said.

Casey ignored him. 'Thanks for the drink, John,' he said, nodding at Stark.

'You ain't just walking away,' Hudson said. His clenched hand was shaking now, his face red.

'Yeah I am. I'm yellow, don't forget.' That raised a few smiles around the room where everyone had been watching the exchange in silence. Later more than one of them would reflect on how the way Casey had spoken and the way he calmly walked past Hudson, brushing off the man's hand as he tried to grab him suggested anything but yellow.

'Where you going?' Hudson said, spinning round to follow Casey.

'I've come to see a young lady,' Casey said, and was at

the bottom of the stairs before any of them saw Suzie up there.

'Suzie Cobb?' he said, catching the girl around the waist as she came down the stairs, turning her, pointing her back the way she'd come.

'My, you're in a hurry,' she said. 'Don't I even get a dance?'

'The piano-player's nervous – he keeps stopping.'

She glanced over her shoulder but Casey pressed a hand into the small of her back.

'What's the rush, cowboy?'

'Instinct,' he said.

And then from down below Milton's voice rose up.

'Hey, Yellow. You hold on. I been waiting on Suzie for half an hour.'

'Well it seems you're going to be waiting a little longer now.'

'No. You hold on, Yellow.'

Milton was hurrying across the bar now, heading towards the bottom of the stairs. Casey turned to face him.

'You were too slow, Milton. No hard feelings. Why not try . . .' He nodded in the direction of the redhead who, like everyone else in the room, was watching Casey and Milton with interest.

'Polly-Anne,' the redhead said.

'It's Suzie I've been waiting for.' Milton had started up the stairs.

'You come any further, Milton, and I'll kick you back down,' Casey said. He was standing above Milton, his stance wide and well balanced. A few people in the bar were smiling. This was fine entertainment and it seemed this young fellow who'd come to pick up his dead father was getting less and less yellow by the minute. Milton hesitated, thought about it for a moment, then took another

21

step up. 'I'll do it, Milton,' Casey said.

Milton's mouth opened but no words came out. Casey saw the man's hand clawing instinctively for his gun.

'Sure, you can shoot me,' Casey said. 'Killing an unarmed man always goes down well with the marshal. I assume you do have a marshal?'

'Marshal Horn,' Suzie said from behind him. 'What's going on?'

'Yeah, what's going on?' Hudson said, also walking towards the bottom of the stairs.

'I just want a few quiet moments alone with the lady.'

'Why?'

'Why do you think?'

'Why didn't *you* go with Polly?' Hudson asked.

'Suzie's been recommended to me,' Casey said, and winked. 'No offence, ma'am,' he added, looking down at Polly-Anne.

'None taken.'

'You have to come down the stairs sometime, Yellow,' Milton said.

'Of course I'll be back down. I've not finished my beer yet.' That made John Stark smile.

'You can laugh now,' Hudson said. 'See how you feel later.'

Suddenly Milton blurted out: 'Don't *say* anything, Suzie. You know what I mean.'

Suzie was looking scared now. She turned to Casey. 'Listen, maybe it'll be better if I pass,' she said.

Casey shook his head, and took her arm. 'It won't hurt, I promise.'

'I don't know.'

'It's OK,' he said, moving upwards, pulling her gently before she had chance to resist.

She led him to a small room at the far end of the landing. As soon as the door closed behind them Casey picked up the only chair that was in the room and wedged it beneath the door handle. It might have been his imagination but he thought he heard footsteps on the landing outside. It was cold inside the small room. A bed lay unmade against one wall. There was a small dressing table with a mirror, some make-up brushes and a lamp on it. In the far wall was a single window covered by a poorly fitting curtain.

'What was all that about?'

'Nothing. Me and Milton just got off on the wrong foot.'

'Who are you?'

'Casey Angelo.' There was no recognition from her. But already she was looking at the door nervously. She knew something was up – Milton's words had hit home. 'You look frightened,' Casey said.

'Why did you put the chair against the door?'

'I didn't want Milton busting in?'

'You think he might?'

'I don't know.' The truth was he figured Milton would be listening at the door. Whether or not he'd try and come in probably depended on how the conversation inside went. They couldn't know that Casey had already learned that Suzie might be worth talking to. If they forced their way in then it would be tantamount to admitting that she was a witness to something. 'What do *you* think?'

She picked at her fingernails nervously.

'I don't know. Why would he?'

'You tell me.'

'I guess he's getting anxious. You were in a hurry yourself.'

Casey nodded. 'It's cold,' he said. 'Might be best if you got into bed.'

She looked at him as if trying to figure this mysterious young stranger out.

'It's five dollars,' she said.

'Five dollars?'

'Yep.'

'*Five* dollars?'

'I'm worth it.'

'I'll give you two.' If anyone was listening from outside surely they'd expect him to try and beat such a price down.

She pretended to spit. 'It's five dollars, cowboy. You were mighty keen outside.' Still she kept glancing at the door but nobody had battered their way in yet – or even tried the handle – and now the thought of five dollars was distracting her.

Casey smiled. She was wise. She understood that when a man rushed up the stairs the way Casey had she had the upper hand in any bargaining.

'Five dollars, it is then.' He gave her the coins and she dropped them into a small bag she had hidden inside the folds of the top half of her dress. Now she started to unbutton the dress.

'You too,' she said.

'Ladies first.'

He stood there watching her getting undressed. She was a pretty girl. Not a beauty for sure. But then beautiful women who were prepared to sell themselves wouldn't be found in a two-bit saloon on the edge of town. If there were any such women in Tyburn Ridge they'd be in a parlour house somewhere and his five dollars wouldn't even get him through the door. But Suzie had a good figure, nice curves, smooth white legs. No sign of the bitterness or the getting-used-up that Martha Slade had referred to.

'You look awfully young,' she said, turning her back on him.

'I'm twenty.'

'Are you shy?' She was slipping into the bed now, pulling the covers up to her neck, shivering.

'No. I'm not shy.'

'Then come on. I ain't got all night.'

He sat on the edge of her bed.

'Tell me,' he whispered. 'What's this about my father cheating on his wife and getting what he deserved?'

It took a moment for the words to sink in. Suddenly she was twisting the covers tight to her neck, realizing that Casey wasn't quite the customer she had thought he was.

'What are you talking about?'

'You know something about my father.'

'I don't even know *you*. How would I know your father?'

'When was the last time you pleasured Milton Craig?' he asked, hoping the sudden change of tack might confuse her enough to let something escape.

'What?'

Jake Bowers and Clifford Tanner had found his father's body last Sunday. It was Wednesday now. Casey took a wild guess.

'Monday or Tuesday?' he suggested.

'What business is it of yours?'

He stared at her, letting his eyes fill with hardness. She shuddered and tried to twist further away from him.

'Monday or Tuesday?' he asked again.

'Monday,' she said at last.

He nodded. 'And what did Milton say about my father?'

She stared back at him. He could almost see her mind racing, trying to figure out where he was coming from and how dangerous he might be.

'I told you I don't know your father.' She was getting angry now, the initial surprise – and associated fear – just losing their edge. He recalled Martha Slade saying she could be as mean as a rattlesnake.

'Robert Angelo,' he said.

She shook her head.

'Someone shot him last Sunday. Maybe Saturday. Just out of town to the west.' Now there was recognition in her eyes. She glanced at the door. 'What did Milton tell you about it?'

Her eyes flicked from Casey to the door and back again.

'He ain't listening any longer, Suzie. If he was he'd have been in here by now.'

'Why d'you let me take my clothes off if you weren't intending anything?'

'Who says I'm not intending anything?' He was still sitting on her bed. He'd figured her nakedness might make her a little more uncomfortable and willing to talk. Certainly it would prevent her running anywhere.

'I could scream,' she said.

'Suzie, I'm not hurting you. I'm not even touching you. I've paid you way over the odds – though you are a pretty woman. All I'm asking is for you to tell me what you know.'

'I can't.'

'Why?'

'Because he'll . . .'

'He'll what?'

'He'll hurt me.'

'And I won't?'

'If I scream they'll come in and likely shoot you before they even see that you're just sat there.'

He nodded. 'Well, I guess in a way you've told me all I need to know anyway.'

'How d'you mean?'

'I can see you're scared and it don't take a genius to work out who it is you're scared of. All I have to do is let him know you told me everything.'

'You wouldn't!'

'You ever hear of a boy named Tom Murphy?'

'No.'

'Friend of mine when I was about eight.' He ran a finger down Suzie's cheek. She shivered where he touched her. 'Milton cut him right here, and right here. Scar like that don't always look too bad on a fella. Wouldn't do for a girl like you though, would it?'

Her eyes were wet with fear. 'Please. I can't say anything.'

He stood up. 'Well, it was nice spending time with you, Suzie. I'll be making my way downstairs now.'

'Wait!' She sat up, still clutching the blankets to her throat.

'What?'

'I don't know much.'

'But you said he was a cheat and got what he deserved.'

'I didn't mean it.'

'It doesn't matter, Suzie. Just tell me.'

'He'd come to see Violet Ranier,' she said quickly as if somehow the words might race by him and this would all be over.

To Casey it was like being shot. He couldn't ever recall spoken words having such a physical impact on him before. Violet Ranier. *Hudson's mother. Spencer's wife.* Spencer, whom his father had taken to jail and not waited around to see hanged.

'I don't know who shot him,' she said quickly. 'Maybe Violet's current husband. I don't know, honest.'

He took a deep breath, calmed himself again.

'Thanks, Suzie,' he said at last. 'It didn't hurt, did it?'

'You won't tell them, will you?'

'No,' he said.

But less than a day later she was dead.

CHAPTER THREE

'I heard there was a little trouble in Sloppy's last night,' Marshal Horn said to Casey the next morning.

Casey looked at him and shook his head.

'Nothing out of the ordinary, sir.'

Martha had already told Casey all about the marshal – he'd been a cowboy, a buffalo hunter, a soldier for the Union, and finally a lawman. He was a tall grey-haired fellow with a thick moustache and eyes that looked out from beneath bushy brows with a narrowness that came from squinting into the sun for too long. His skin was burnt a deep tan and the lines etched in his face were testament to a man who had long battled the elements. He gave the impression of being a hard man who would suffer no fools gladly. But he was old, too, and Casey couldn't help but think that the town was too big for him, the population outgrowing the man's energy and abilities. Robert Angelo had told Casey that such situations were common all over the territories.

'Towns are growing up fast,' he'd said. 'There's more people, more saloons, more saloon girls, more farmers, more cattle, more guns. All of this means there's more trouble. Yet there ain't always more lawmen. Oh, folks will cotton on eventually but at the moment they just look to their sheriff and his deputy if they're lucky. And sometimes one man – or two – just ain't enough.'

'That's a nasty bruise under your right eye,' Horn said. Martha Slade had said the same thing at breakfast.

'That was the one I didn't see coming.'

'Let's see your knuckles, boy.'

Casey held them up.

'Looks like you connected a couple of times yourself.'

'It was nothing.'

'I heard otherwise.'

Hudson and his gang had been waiting for Casey downstairs in the saloon. Casey had figured as much and was tensed and ready as he came down the stairs. But he'd misjudged their patience. They'd let him walk calmly back to his beer, they'd smiled and nodded, and Campbell had even asked him how Suzie had been.

'My turn now,' Milton had said, and had moved away from the bar. Casey should have sensed then that something was up, but instead he relaxed, picked up his beer and was about to drink up and leave when Milton hit him square in the back with a chair.

It wasn't a good shot. It didn't connect well, and though Casey's legs buckled and he lost his beer all over the bar he didn't go down. After that it was a blur. He turned, tore the chair from Milton's grasp and launched it back at the little man's head. Then Hudson was swinging at him and caught him on the cheek and he replied with two good shots to Hudson's belly before Campbell got behind him and tried to grab his arms. Casey knew that if Campbell – who was the most muscular of them all – caught him and held him fast he was in big trouble, so he stepped backwards on to one of Campbell's feet, pressing it down and holding it fast against the floor, and at the same time he struck backwards with his elbow as hard as he could. The blow caught Campbell in the solar plexus and the redhaired man doubled up. A Chinese rail-worker had shown Casey that move back in the yards at Omaha. Standing on

Campbell's foot meant the big man hadn't been able to move with the blow and had thus absorbed the full force of the elbow in his stomach.

Now Milton was back in his face, fists flying all ways. Casey hit him once on the mouth and that was when he felt the skin on his knuckles split. Then Hudson threw a good one that Casey only saw at the last moment. He swayed out of the way but still took the shot. That made everything a blur and he decided that maybe it was time to retreat towards the door, where breathing heavily, he looked back at Hudson and Milton and Campbell, all three of them bleeding and laughing and calling him yellow. John Stark was standing behind them. He'd taken no part. Instead he just raised his glass to Casey, who stumbled outside where the cold air cut into the scrapes on his face and knuckles like a scalpel.

'We all just got off on the wrong tack, Marshal. I know those boys from a long time back.'

'It might be best to steer clear of them.'

'I'll try.'

Horn nodded but the way he screwed his forehead up told Casey that the man didn't really believe him. 'Now, about your father.'

'Anything you can tell me would be much appreciated.'

'What do you know already?'

'Just that a couple of Franklin Hicks's men found his body in a snowdrift out to the west.'

'Yep. That's about the size of it.'

It was Thursday morning. Casey had slept poorly, bathed his bruises in cold water, eaten a good breakfast and was now in the marshal's office. Already he was starting to get a strong feeling about who had killed his father. All of his instincts, all of his common sense, and all of the history pointed to Hudson and his boys being responsible. But then it was nothing he hadn't already suspected on the train west the day before. However it was all just circumstantial evidence and Casey wanted something firm.

'You must know more than that, Marshal.'

Horn stood up, stretched, grimaced and pressed his hands into the small of his back.

'This goddamn cold weather,' he said. 'I'm sure the winters are colder 'n' longer than they used to be. Coffee?'

Casey nodded. 'Did you go out and look at the scene?'

Horn laughed. 'You've been reading too many dime novels, son. Maybe that's what they do way back East.'

'So you don't know if Hicks's men were even telling the truth?'

Horn picked up the pot off the cast iron stove and filled two tin cups with black coffee. When he turned back his smile was gone.

'I have no reason to doubt those boys, Mr Angelo. There are some fellows in these parts that maybe I wouldn't believe but if Jake and Clifford tell me that they found your father's body where they say they did then that's good enough for me. You want to call them liars then you wait until Saturday and you can call them liars to their faces.'

'That's not what I meant.'

'And I hope they're in a good mood when you do it or else that little scrape you got last night will seem like—'

'Marshal, that's not what I meant.'

'I know what you meant. Son, I know you're upset over your father's death. And you're entitled to be. But it was blowing a blizzard the night they found him. By the time I got out there – if I could have got out there – there would have been another foot of snow. It would have been dark, too. There was nothing to see.' Horn handed him his coffee. 'I don't know what your father was doing back in these parts. I do know he should have stayed away.'

'But you're not investigating?'

Horn gave Casey a fierce look. He opened a tin on his table, took out a cheroot without offering one to Casey, flicked a lucifer with his thumb and lit up. Then he walked over to the window.

'How old are you, son?'

'Twenty.'

'Just a pup.'

Casey didn't say anything. He'd already riled Horn a little and had no wish to antagonize him further. It was always good to have the law on your side.

'With age comes a lot of things – aching bones is one of the worst. But experience . . . there is no short cut to experience, boy. You come in here wanting to know if I've been to the scene of your daddy's shooting on the night of a blizzard, you question my judgement of men I've known for close on ten years, you criticise me for not investigating further—'

'I didn't—'

'It was in your voice, boy.' Horn took a long pull on his cheroot. He stared out of the frosted window, let the smoke ease from his nostrils, then turned to Casey. 'I've got my own ideas about who might have shot your father. I've even – despite what you may think – spoken to a few people. I'm a good lawman, Casey. But people in this town don't give much away and until they do I'm afraid there's nothing I can do. And I don't say that lightly. I say that because I've been doing this job for a long time. *Experience*, Casey. Don't criticize me because of it.'

Casey took a sip of coffee, then he pulled a leather pouch from his pocket and started making a cigarette of his own. He didn't smoke a great deal like some guys. But once in a while it was a calming thing to do – both making the cigarette and smoking it. Something the marshal had said had brought back Hap's words of yesterday: *We could do with a lawman like your father round these parts again.* It was possible Horn had heard such opinions expressed around town. No wonder he got sore at being criticized by a young stranger. And if that stranger was the son of the lawman that folks talked about in hallowed tones then it would make the criticism even harder to bear.

Horn watched Casey rolling up his cigarette. There was a long silence between them. Eventually Horn said:

'I'm sorry, I should have offered you one.' His voice was still stony. He walked across to the table and pushed the box of cheroots towards Casey. Casey noticed that the marshal limped slightly. Maybe it was the cold weather and aching bones or maybe an old wound. Whatever it was, it slowed him down a little.

'No, *I'm* sorry,' Casey said. 'I didn't mean to make you mad.'

Horn nodded. The awkward moment was over.

'It's OK. I guess I get frustrated sometimes at what folks can get away with. I wish I could help you more.'

Though Casey would have preferred to smoke his own cigarette rather than the foul smelling type that Horn had offered he put his own aside and lit up one of the cheroots, downed the remains of his coffee and then asked Horn how he would be able to recognize the spot where his father had been found, were he to want to go out there himself. Horn gave him some directions, a couple of landmarks and recounted the brief description that Jake Bowers and Clifford Tanner had given him.

'Not sure I'd recommend heading out there on a day like this. And you likely won't find anything anyway,' he warned.

'I'm not looking for anything, Marshal. I just want to see the spot where my father died.'

Horn nodded again. For a moment his eyes appeared unfocused.

'My father went to fight the Mexicans. He never came

home. I don't know what happened to him. Never heard a word. If he were still alive he'd be in his eighties now. I can understand why you want to see that place. But you keep an eye on the weather. Round these parts it can turn and bite you quicker than a lady rattler.'

Casey stood up. 'Just one more thing, Marshal.'

'What's that?'

'Who's the best shot in Tyburn Ridge?'

'The best shot?'

'There must be some marksmen in town.'

Horn nodded as he cottoned on to Casey's line of thinking.

'I saw your daddy's body, too, son. You can't hang someone just because they're a good shot.'

'I'm just curious.'

'There are probably only a dozen men in town or on the nearby ranges that I'd call marksmen. A lot more would give themselves that title. And the number rises if you start to take into account lucky shots. More than one reputation has been built on a lucky shot. You don't know how far away the killer was, either. It might not have needed a marksman.'

'Hudson Ranier?'

'Don't start jumping to conclusions.'

'I'm just interested.'

'He blackens your eye one night and the next morning you have him lined up for murder. Talk like that outside of these walls and you'll be lying in the snow just like your father was. I'm sorry if that sounds harsh.'

'So he is a dangerous man, then?'

'You're putting words in my mouth, Casey.'

'Only because you're not putting them there yourself.'

Horn smiled thinly. 'You're like a rabbit dog, ain't you? You just don't quit.'

Case smiled back. 'Well?'

'Hudson Ranier likes his revolvers. Up close he's dangerous.'

'But not a marksman?'

'I didn't say that.'

'Any of the others?'

'Others?'

'Hudson's gang.'

The marshal sighed. 'I take it back. You're worse'n a rabbit dog.'

'Milton Craig?'

The marshal laughed. 'Milton's a danger only to himself. With a gun anyway. He's got a reputation for being cruel with a knife.'

'I remember.'

'No, the only one of Hudson's boys who I'd describe as being a marksman is John Stark.'

When Casey left the marshal's office Milton Craig was across the frozen street. He was walking along the plank-walk smoking hard on a cigarette and jumped nervously when the marshal's door opened. Their eyes met. Casey paused for a moment and then nodded.

'Milton.'

Milton swallowed. 'What you been doing in the marshal's office, Yellow?' There was an anxiety in his voice that Casey hadn't noticed previously. He put it down to this being the first time he had seen Milton alone without the protection of the others.

'Just getting his opinion on a few things, Milton.'

Milton glanced up and down the street. Casey followed his gaze. A stagecoach was being readied at the hotel, several horses were tied to the rail outside Sloppy's, a freight wagon was being unloaded at the general store, and a small black dog was scratching at the door of the barbershop. Other than that there was little sign of life.

Thick grey clouds, heavy with sleet, had rolled in over night and though this cover had raised the temperature slightly a bitter norther was adding a wind-chill factor to the equation and most folks that didn't have to be outside weren't.

'What things would they be, Yellow?'

'I just asked him if he had any idea who killed my father.'

Now Milton moved to the edge of the far plank-walk. His eyes were still darting all ways as if he was desperate to see everyone who might be around.

'And did he?'

'We had an interesting discussion, Milton.'

Milton looked across at the marshal's office before glancing back at Casey again.

'You looking for your buddies, Milton?' Casey said.

'No.' Milton took a last draw on his cigarette then dropped the remainder on to the plank walk where he ground it out beneath his heel. 'You know, it might be better if you just took your daddy's body and went home, Yellow.'

Casey smiled to himself. This was the man who last night had smashed a chair against his back. Today he appeared even smaller than normal.

'Not sure I could live with myself if I did that, Milton. I'm sure you understand.'

Milton shivered. He cupped his hands and blew on them.

'Just offering some advice,' he said.

'You wouldn't know anything about it, would you?'

'About your daddy?'

'Yep.'

'Why d'you ask that?'

Casey shrugged. 'No reason. Just curious.'

'Listen Yellow, you ain't welcome round these parts

anyway. And all these questions are liable to make it worse. Why don't you just up and go?'

'Funny, yesterday at the station you all seemed pleased to see me. Was a welcoming party and everything.'

'Yeah, well that was Hud's idea. Way I see it your daddy shouldn't have come back in the first place and now neither should you.'

Casey nodded. 'Well you'll be rid of me soon enough. A few more days should do it.'

Milton spat into the snow. 'Sooner the better.'

'So tell me, Milton. Where can I hire me a buggy and a guide?'

'What?'

Casey smiled. 'It's time for me to go and see where my father got shot.'

'Why you asking me?'

'Actually, I'm just letting you know where I'll be. That way you mightn't feel obliged to follow me.'

'I wasn't following you.'

'You know, the marshal reckons I'm like a rabbit dog.'

'Huh?'

'He says I just don't quit. And you know something, Milton?'

'What?'

'He's right. I'm not intending quitting until I find out who killed my father.'

'Then what?'

'Justice, Milton. Justice. Isn't that the right thing to do? An eye for an eye. You must have heard of that.'

Casey wandered down to the stables where he found the proprietor, Nez Sully, reluctant to hire him a horse.

'Just for a few hours,' Casey said.

'I don't hire out,' Sully told him. 'These aren't even my horses.' He was a thin wiry man with a black moustache

37

and beard flecked with grey. He chewed tobacco constantly and showed a huge reluctance to move away from the stove, only doing so when it was time to spit out the tobacco juice. Casey wondered why he didn't simply move the spittoon across the room next to the stove.

'None of 'em? Not even one?'

Sully curled up the corner of his lip.

'Maybe one of 'em is mine. But that don't meantersay I want to hire her out.'

'It's just for an hour or two.'

'There's a blizzard coming. I just got 'em all rubbed down and settled in.'

Casey doubted any of the horses had been out already that morning.

'I'll be back before the blizzard hits. How much would it take to persuade you?'

'I tol' you. I don't hire out.'

'Five dollars?'

'I tol' you . . . *five dollars*?'

'Five dollars.'

'And you'll be back before the snow hits.'

'Uh-huh.'

'How do I know you'll be back at all?'

'You have my word.'

'I don't mean to be rude but—'

'I understand. Why don't you go down the street and ask Marshal Horn if I'm a trustworthy fellow. Or Hap Smith.'

Sully held his hands out towards the stove. He didn't want to go out into the stables let alone down the street.

'Hap Smith?' he said. 'You had dealings with Hap?'

'It's why I'm here.'

Now Sully started to look nervous as well as reluctant.

'Look, I don't know.'

'Five dollars.'

'And where is it you said you wanted to go?'

'It's where the west trail takes a turn to the north and then about twenty yards further up it twists left again. There's a rock fall there they had to work around.'

'Aye. I know the place. What you want to go there for?'

'That's where my father was shot dead.'

Sully swallowed in surprise and then immediately started coughing. His eyes watered and he had to bend forward whilst he retched. He reached out blindly for support and his right hand came to rest on the stove. He yelped and coughed and was now holding the scorched hand deep in his left armpit whilst he hopped around in pain.

'I think you just caused him to swallow his tobacco,' someone said from the doorway behind Casey. He turned. It was a girl in a buckskin hat and a heavy brown coat. Black hair tumbled from beneath the hat and striking blue eyes looked steadily upon him.

'So long as he doesn't choke before I've finalized this deal,' Casey said.

'I know the place you're talking about,' the girl said. Then she smiled and added: 'Casey Angelo.'

There was something familiar about her – the high cheekbones, full lips and smooth skin – and yet he couldn't place her. Despite the familiarity he was sure he wouldn't have forgotten such a girl if ever he had known her.

'How do you know my name?' he asked, puzzled yet pleased that he was known to such a beautiful girl.

'I swam naked with you in Jagged Creek,' she said and flashed him a wide smile that caused his heart to flutter. 'I never forget a man I've swum naked with.'

Now the familiarity started to take shape.

'Sam,' he said. 'Sam Ranier.' She looked now like her mother had looked back when he was a kid. Even as a six-year-old he had somehow recognized that Violet Ranier had been one of the prettiest women in Tyburn Ridge.

'The one and only,' she said. 'It's good to see you again, Casey.'

He could only stand and stare, speechless, his heart over the fluttering and now racing instead. His vision blurred momentarily and it was just as if Violet Ranier was there in front of him. Violet Ranier, whom his father had come to see and maybe had been shot because of it.

'You're not trying to raise a picture of me naked in the creek, are you, Casey Angelo?'

He shook his head. His vision cleared. His heartbeat slowed.

'I'm sorry. I didn't recognize you.'

She smiled again. 'I'll forgive you. I heard about your father, Casey. I'm sorry.'

He nodded. Her smile was wonderful and her looks breathtaking and now old memories were rushing to the forefront of his mind. But somewhere inside an alarm bell started ringing. *She's Hudson's little sister*, the bell warned insistently. *Violet's daughter. Maybe you should be thinking about treading very carefully right now* .

Behind them Sully was wiping his eyes and standing straight again.

'Five dollars,' he said again. 'And you'll be back in an hour?'

'I can show Mr Angelo the place he wants to see,' Sam said. 'It's on my way home. He won't get lost.' Casey was wondering if she knew what Suzie Cobb knew: that his father had been killed on the way to see her mother.

It took them forty-five minutes to get from the wooden sign marking Tyburn Ridge's limit to the bend in the trail where someone had ambushed and killed Robert Angelo. Forty-five minutes instead of the twenty that Hap had described because the ground was frozen and treacherous and Sam was leading a pack-horse weighed down with provisions. It

40

took them forty-five minutes because the horse that Sully had hired to Casey had seen its best days some fifteen years before and an icy wind was blowing into their faces, bringing flurries of snow and finding every tear and joint in their clothes. But most of all it took them forty-five minutes because they rode slowly, almost oblivious to the weather, talking and, despite the occasion, laughing occasionally and catching up on old times. If Casey had thought about it he would have noted the irony that it was only on the way to see his father's dying-ground that he was able to put the pain of his father's death aside for a few moments.

Sam had been one of his best friends for a while back in the old days and she was anxious to know what life was like in Omaha, and what adventures Casey had got up to since he had left. Likewise he was keen to know all about her. Yet when the conversation turned to her family Casey suddenly felt awkward. After all, it had been his father who had arrested her father. An arrest that had led to her father being hanged.

'It's all right,' she said.

'No it's not.'

'It was a long time ago. My father . . .' she sighed and he wished he hadn't brought the subject up. 'He wasn't a good man. To be honest I don't remember that much about him. I know . . . I know he hurt Mama. I mean, he didn't hit her. But he hurt her in other ways.'

'I shouldn't have mentioned it. I'm sorry. Let's—'

'No, it needs to be said.'

'But don't you see? I . . .' He let the words tail off.

'You what?' She was riding alongside him, heavy coat obscuring the curves of her body, a scarf and hat hiding much of her face, but he could see her dark and intense eyes staring at him and he could just see her mouth, straight now, no sign of the laughter and joy that had been on her lips for the first forty minutes of their journey.

He had to be honest. 'I hate the man – the men, maybe – who killed my father. I don't know who they are but I hate them.' Now the alarm bell was ringing again, this time furiously. Was he really being honest? Could it be her brother he was talking about?

Her eyes were compassionate.

'Casey, I'm sure I hated your father for a while, too. I know my mama did. And my brother. But that was a long time ago and I believe – I *know* – that he was only doing his job. My father was a murderer, Casey. And a . . .' She let the words hang.

'It's OK. You don't have to talk about it.'

She was silent for a moment, eyes fixed ahead at the distant mountains, the dark sky and the coming storm.

'No,' she said eventually. 'Maybe we should change the subject.'

He reached out a hand towards her.

'I'm sorry.'

They were close enough to touch. The contact – leather glove upon leather glove – somehow seemed to warm him and he wondered if it was doing the same to her or whether it was just his imagination. It seemed impossible that he could really feel anything through all that cowhide, yet he really did sense warmth coming through. He decided to ask her about the Ranier's ranch.

'Who's in charge of the Bar H now?'

She shook her head. Another tender subject. Then before he could say another word she said:

'Casey. This is the place.'

He couldn't help but think that there ought to be more to it. His father had been killed here. It ought to be more than just a twist in the trail, an old rock fall, and a couple of trees struggling to stay alive in the shelter of the cliff. This place would surely become – maybe already had become – one of the defining locations of his life. Certainly it had become such for his father. Maybe Casey would come back another day and erect a cross, a monument, something. Even a pile of stones carefully constructed to withstand the wind and the rain, the winter freeze, and the summer sandstorms would show that *something* happened here. Something of note. But for now it was just a frozen twist in the trail, cloaked with snow.

He dismounted and handed his reins to Sam. The frozen snow crackled beneath his boots. He looked up at the rocks. Was that where they had been hiding? He turned and looked to his right. There were boulders there. Maybe they had been hiding behind those. The first bullet had hit his father in the left hand side of his chest and the second across to the right. If his father had been riding in the same direction as Casey and Sam were heading that would mean the killer was up in the rocks. If he had been coming the other way – if he had already seen Sam's mother – then the boulders would make more sense.

He looked up at Sam. She had pulled her scarf up over her mouth. All he could see were her eyes. The snow was settling on her shoulders.

'Do you know whereabouts he was found?'

She shook her head.

'Listen,' he said. 'I think I'm going to take a look around. You'll freeze to death if you just sit there. Why don't you get on your way?' Part of him – a big part – didn't want her to leave, there seemed to be so much more to talk about. And that brief touch of gloved hands was like the first shot of good whiskey after a long ride, it warmed him and made him shiver with delight, and he couldn't help but want more. Yet another part of him wanted to be alone.

She pulled down the scarf.

'Everything's covered in snow.'

'I know. I just need to do it.'

'What are you hoping to find?'

'I don't know. Something. Anything. Nothing, I expect. I just need to be thorough.'

'Thorough?'

'For my own peace of mind.'

She looked at him and frowned slightly.

'You're a strange one, Casey Angelo.'

He smiled and ice that had frozen on his lips cracked.

'Thank you for bringing me here.'

'What did you mean: 'thorough'?'

'I just meant . . . I just want to know as much about what happened to my father as possible.'

'What are you planning to do, Casey?'

'Nothing.' He knew she could see the lie in his face. They stared at each other for a long cold moment. 'Nothing,' he said again, softer this time.

Her silence went on a little longer.

'I don't want you to get hurt,' she said, eventually.

'I won't. I promise.' He glanced up at the rock face. He was imagining someone up there, looking down the barrel of a rifle. It had been snowing – or at least bitterly cold – the day his father was killed. Whoever had been up there must have been dressed up warm. They must have been waiting for quite a while. There might be some sign of them there.

'You're not going to climb up there, are you?'

He nodded.

'Casey, it's frozen. One slip and you could break your neck. If you broke a leg that would be just as bad in this weather.'

'I'll be all right.'

'I'll wait.'

'No. You'll freeze.'

'I'll wait,' she said, and pulled her scarf back up over her mouth.

*

44

He wandered over to the boulders on the ground. There was no sign of anyone having been there. But that didn't mean no one had been. The snow was thick and crusted with ice. It was impossible to tell anything from looking at the ground surrounding the boulders. He pursed his lips, shook his head at Sam, and then turned towards the rock face across the trail. From a distance it looked sheer, but once closer Casey could see several ways of climbing at least part way up. Wind erosion and cracks where water had collected, frozen, and split the rock had created scores of handholds and ledges. He briefly removed a glove and reached out and touched the stone. It was cold but not slippery. He walked to the left, then to the right, looking for an easy way up. And sure enough here was another rock fall – several boulders resting on top of one another – which had created a series of steps upwards. The shale on top of the first boulder was loose but he steadied himself against the rock face and stepped up again, then a third time, finding a crack in the rock wall into which he could slip his gloved hand to heave himself higher. The rock he now found himself on suddenly shifted beneath his weight and he had to stand still for a moment whilst it steadied beneath him. He looked down at Sam. Already he was fifteen feet above her. Were he an assassin it would be an easy shot from up here. Someone riding through the pass would have nowhere to hide. One of the horses snorted and fidgeted. He could see Sam's breath frosting in the air and decided he should hurry. He looked down at the rock beneath him. There was just a thin layer of white on these sheltered rocks. But there was no evidence of anyone else having been here. Now he looked upwards. There was another reasonably big rock above him that he ought to be able to get on top of. From where he stood it looked like it had a flat top and angled gently upwards. A perfect place for someone to lie in wait. He found a foothold and a handhold, pulled himself up as far as he could, reached for the top of the rock and pushed upwards with his foot, managed to get his chest and arms on top of the rock. Now he pulled himself on to the flat slab and just for a moment he was helpless in the arms of mother nature. If the rock was as precariously balanced as the one below it could tilt over, slip him off, and then come crashing down upon him. He held his breath. The rock held firm. It was about four feet wide and six long. Flat and smooth. And as he lay there he realized he couldn't see Sam and thus she couldn't see him.

This was perfect. This was the place.

He sat up and looked around on top of the rock. Nothing. He took off a glove again and ran his fingers along the bottom edge of the rock. Still nothing. And now disappointment started to rise within. This time the feeling was like bad whiskey, rotgut, making him feel hot and sick. What had he expected? A signed card? *Hudson was here?* Though hadn't the marshal said that John Stark was the marksman? He breathed in deeply, calming himself. A cigarette end, a matchstick, anything would have been good but there was nothing. Maybe there had been and maybe the wind had carried it away. Maybe he was simply too late. He turned and looked out along the trail. This was the place. Someone had lain right here and had waited for his father. And then they had killed him. But who? And why?

As he climbed down off the rock he knew he had to see her again. She'd remained there, motionless, in the snow all the while he was up there, and even though his mind was racing with ideas, with disappointment, he also felt a hope and a warmth and an excitement inside and he knew that that was because of her.

'Can I meet you again?' he asked. He feared his words might sound clumsy or abrupt but he knew he had to get them out or it might be too late. This close he could see she was so cold that her arms were shaking uncontrollably. He should have insisted that she ride on home. When he breathed it felt like slivers of ice sliding down his throat. 'I can come out to the Bar H,' he said. 'Is it just a case of following this trail?'

She nodded. 'How long are you here for?'

'I don't know. A few days.'

'It's not long.'

He felt that he could almost read her mind. Or at least part of it. *I'd like to see you again, Casey. But what's the point? You're about to leave. Again.*

'I can always come back,' he said. And he meant it. The excitement and warmth and hope that she had ignited within him, the touch of their gloved fingertips, the way her smooth skin glistened and her eyes flashed and the way she had teased him about swimming naked with him all came together inside him and he knew he would readily come back to see her again. But what of all the unknowns? She was beautiful. Surely there was a young man on the horizon. And why hadn't she wanted to talk about the Bar H? It was her mother his father had supposedly returned to see. What was that all about? And, worst of all, what would happen if it turned out that it had been Hudson lying on that flat rock above them, looking down a rifle at Robert Angelo?

'What do you mean?' she asked him, but there was no way he could put all of his feelings into words.

'Nothing. Look, you're freezing. What say I ride out tomorrow?'

'You don't have a horse.'

'I'll find one.'

'I can come to town.'

'No, there's no need for that.'

'I do it all the time, Casey. It's only an hour or less.

Anyway, it gets me out.'

'No, I insist. I'll come to the ranch. About midday.'

The weather was his ally for once. She was too cold to argue.

'OK.' She smiled and pulled her scarf back up. Then they touched gloves again and it was as good as the first time.

Back at the stables Sully asked him if he had found the place. Casey nodded and explained what had happened.

'And was there anything up there?' Sully asked.

Casey was about to say no when something, instinct maybe, made him think again.

'Yes,' he said. 'Matter of fact, I did find something.'

Sully's eyes widened.

'What?'

'I think it's best I don't say. I need to tell the marshal.'

With that he left Sully open mouthed and headed out the door only to run straight into the very man they had just been talking about.

'I need to talk to you, Casey,' Horn said. His expression gave nothing away but his voice was as cold as the day. 'I had my doubts we'd be seeing you again. I wondered if that was all an act earlier.'

'What?'

'You know a young lady by the name of Suzie Cobb?'

'Yes. I met her last night.'

'Some boys from Sloppy's say that you were *with* her last night.'

'We talked, that was all. Why?'

'She's over at Hap's right now. Someone cut her throat last night and everyone I've spoken to says you were the last man up there.'

CHAPTER FOUR

Casey stared at the marshal, his mind racing. There were too many emotions to make sense of, too much to take in. He shook his head. 'No,' was all he could say.

The marshal nodded.

'Yes,' he said. Then added: 'You want to step inside my office for a few minutes?'

He followed the marshal along the plank-walk. There were a few people about but he didn't know if they were looking at him or not. He hardly saw them. They were just shapes on the outside of the tunnel vision that had arisen from nowhere and darkened his world even further. He hadn't *physically* killed Suzie Cobb but she was dead because of him. Of that he had no doubt. He had questioned her and Milton had known it. Now she was dead. Goddamn, why hadn't he been a bit more discreet?

'What happened?' he asked, as soon as they were in the marshal's office.

Horn turned on him. 'You tell me, son.'

Horn wandered over to the stove and poured himself a coffee. This time he didn't offer Casey one. Casey stared at the steaming liquid and shivered. During the ride back to town the blizzard had worsened and he was freezing right through to his bones. But he was darned if he was going to ask for a cup of coffee no matter how cold he was.

'I heard that Suzie might know something about my

father, that was all.'

Horn looked at him. The man's narrow eyes looked as hard as stone now. They were perfectly still, too, unblinking, unmoving. Casey felt as if he was a buffalo in the sights of Horn's rifle. Horn said nothing but let the uncomfortable silence linger, waiting for Casey to fill it. Casey didn't and eventually Horn said:

'That ain't all. Tell me everything.'

So Casey told him how he'd gone into Sloppy's, narrowly avoided a fight with Hudson, had a chat with Suzie, and then ended up having the fight anyway, which Horn already knew about.

'And what did Suzie tell you?'

'She said my father had come to town to see Violet Ranier.'

Horn nodded.

'You knew that?' Casey asked.

'No.'

'I didn't kill her, Marshal.'

'How did Suzie Cobb come by this information?'

'Milton Craig.'

'And Milton was in Sloppy's last night?'

'Yes.'

'And he saw you go upstairs with Suzie?'

'Yes.'

The marshal sighed. Now he wandered back over to the coffee-pot, poured a cup for Casey and held it out to him. Casey took the hot drink gratefully.

'You mightn't have done that poor girl any favours acting the way you did.'

'I know.'

'She didn't come down after you'd spoken to her?'

Casey shook his head. 'She was scared.'

'With good reason.'

'I didn't kill her, Marshal.'

Horn lifted his hat up, ran a hand through his grey hair and shook his head. 'You might as well have done, boy.'

'You know who did it, don't you.'

'No one saw anyone go upstairs except you.'

'You know it wasn't me!'

'I know that you came into town yesterday and before you'd even been here one evening you had yourself a fight and now a girl's dead.'

'What did you mean outside when you said you wondered if it was an all act earlier?'

The marshal sighed.

'I like to think I'm a good judge of character, son. I mightn't be so quick these days but age and experience is worth a lot. I know what you're here to do. I'm no fool. I just have to figure out whether or not you'd cut a girl's throat to get the information you wanted.'

'No. I didn't. I wouldn't.' Outside the blizzard was thickening. The whiteness beyond the window seemed to close them in. This room, the stove, the desk, the coffee, the posters on the wall, the door to the cages out back were his whole world. He felt helpless and yet ever more determined. Whoever had killed his father had now killed Suzie and was trying to pin it on him. He clenched his hands hard around the tin coffee-cup and felt it bend slightly out of shape beneath his anger.

'Casey, I probably shouldn't say this, but I believe you. The question is, what should I do?'

'You know who did it,' Casey said again.

'No. *You* think *you* know. And maybe you're right. But there's a darn sight more evidence pointing your way than anyone else's.'

'Is there another set of stairs up to Suzie's room?'

The marshal nodded.

'As good as. An old woman would find it easy enough to climb up there the back way.'

'Then—'

'I know. I know. And before you ask I had a look round there and there's no sign of anyone climbing up there. That doesn't mean they didn't. The snow that was on the window-ledge has fallen off.'

'Or been brushed off,' Casey said, then added, 'Was the window open?'

'Casey, you want to do my job for me, how about telling me what I should do with you?'

Casey took a sip of coffee.

'I didn't do it,' he said.

'I believe you.'

'Then . . .'

'Upholding the law in a place like this is a funny business, Casey. Sometimes you have to do something even though it's wrong.'

'What do you mean?'

'I mean, I'm thinking maybe I should lock you up.'

'What?'

'See, the way it looks to the townsfolk is that more'n likely you did it. They don't have the benefit of my experience. If I lock you up they'll be happy. Then maybe in a day or two, I'll let you go. By then I'll be able to convince them that I know it wasn't you.'

It was all wrong. It shouldn't be happening this way. He thought of his father riding out to see a woman who wasn't his wife. He thought of someone lying on a rock and taking aim at his father's heart. He pictured his father frozen in a coffin outside Hap's. He hadn't come here to be locked up. He'd come here to find answers and. . .

Now a picture of Sam burst into Casey's mind. He could see her sat at the kitchen table with her hair pinned up and a beautiful smile on her face and he could see himself sitting across from her. Maybe their hands would be touching over the table. He was meant to see her tomorrow.

52

'You can't lock up an innocent man.'

'See, I don't know that you're innocent, do I?'

'But you said—'

'I said, I believe you. It's not the same as knowing, Casey.'

Casey stood up. The coffee-cup was on the table and both his fists were clenched now.

'This is crazy.'

'Sit down, son. You try and make a run for it and even if you get out the door you'll have half the town after you. You ain't got a horse and in this weather you'll freeze to death in a few hours.'

'You should be talking to Milton Craig, Marshal. You told me yourself that he's the knifeman round these parts.'

'Casey—'

'You know who was hanging around outside this morning, Marshal?'

'Who?'

'Milton Craig. He was as nervous as hell, too.'

'You know, maybe you should consider that me locking you up might be the best thing for you. The way it feels to me is that if you're walking around town talking like this I might have another body on my hands sooner rather than later.'

'I can look after myself.'

Horn nodded. 'I don't doubt that.' Now he reached across his desk and took a cheroot out of the box there. 'Want one?'

Casey shook his head. 'No, thanks.' The one he'd tried earlier had been a bad enough experience. He watched Horn light up, suck deeply, exhale a mouthful of foul-smelling smoke into the previously clean air between the two of them, and then sigh. Whether Horn had planned it this way or not the long pause seemed to work. Slowly

Casey unclenched his fists.

'I think maybe it's time for you to just leave, Casey,' Horn said.

'Leave?'

'Leave town.'

Casey thought of his father again. And again he thought of someone lying on the flat piece of rock aiming a gun at his father's heart. This time the gunman had a face. It was Hudson Ranier. But even as the image formed in his mind the face changed and it was John Stark, the marksman. Then a new picture came to him, Suzie Cobb undressing in front of him. He thought of how scared she'd been and how he had tricked her into talking to him. Then he thought of Milton Craig climbing up to her window, slipping it open, easing himself inside and cutting Suzie's throat. And with this thought came an almost overwhelming guilt.

'No,' Casey said.

'Maybe you don't have that choice, Casey. Maybe I'll make it for you. There's an eastbound train tomorrow morning. I want you on it.'

'Marshal—'

'No arguing, Casey. The only question is whether I lock you up in the meantime.'

The marshal stared at him through the cigarette smoke and Casey waited for him to make a decision.

CHAPTER FIVE

That night Casey lay awake in his bed at Martha Slade's boarding-house and tried to make sense of everything that had happened. The marshal had eventually relented and agreed not to lock Casey up provided he went straight back to Martha's, kept a very low profile, and was on the eastbound train in the morning.

'If you're not on that train, Casey,' he said, 'I *will* lock you up. I'll lock you up and I'll put you on the next train myself. I mean it, son.'

But already Casey had broken the marshal's first condition – he hadn't gone directly back to Martha's. Instead he had called in on Hap.

'Here's someone I didn't expect to see,' Hap said, pushing his glasses up away from his eyes as if not believing what they were showing him. 'I was half-wondering what to do with your father.'

'How do you mean?' Casey said, brushing snow from his sleeves.

'The word is that you were responsible for . . .' Hap nodded in the direction of his backroom. 'Suzie Cobb.'

Casey nodded. 'The marshal's just been grilling me. I didn't do it, Hap.'

'I know that, Casey. But when's the truth ever got in the way of making folks feel better?'

'Can I see her?'

Hap nodded. 'Want a whiskey first? Or after?'

'After.'

Hap led Casey into his back room. With the blizzard blowing outside it was dark and Hap had several kerosene lanterns burning. In the middle of the room an open coffin lay on top of a long trestle-table.

'We're going to bury her Saturday,' Hap said as Casey walked towards the coffin. 'Won't be much fuss. I doubt there'll be many folks there to see her lowered down. A lot of her "friends" won't want their wives to know they had anything to do with Suzie.' There was a sadness in his voice and when Casey looked across at him he saw it in the undertaker's shadowed face too.

Hap had buttoned Suzie's nightdress right up to her throat but even so the jagged fatal wound was still partly visible. Casey felt a sadness of his own rising. Tears welled in his eyes and guilt flared in his chest. Suzie looked like she was sleeping. Eyes closed, skin white and still. He reached into the coffin and laid a finger on her cheek just as a tear rolled down his own.

'I'm sorry,' he whispered. Then he turned to Hap. 'It was my fault,' he said. 'I didn't kill her but I'm to blame as sure as winter's cold.'

Hap was holding his spectacles in his hand, polishing them. Now he looked up at Casey.

'Don't be silly, Casey.'

'I questioned her, Hap. Martha said that Suzie knew something about my father. I questioned her and now she's dead.'

'That doesn't make you responsible.'

'She wouldn't be dead if I hadn't done that.'

'Maybe not. But you can take that line of thinking back as far as you like. Maybe Martha's to blame for telling you about Suzie.'

'Don't be silly.'

'Maybe I'm to blame for suggesting you stay at Martha's.'

'That's nonsense, Hap.'

'And so is blaming yourself.'

'I know who did it.'

'You do?'

'Milton Craig.'

'You have proof?'

'No.'

'Then you shouldn't go round saying such things.'

'They killed my father, too. I'm sure of it.'

'They?'

'Milton. Hudson. Campbell James. John Stark.'

'Casey, you be careful now. You're upset and angry. Don't do anything silly.'

'It won't be silly.'

'I don't want to be burying you, too.'

'Don't worry, Hap. You won't be. Keep a few coffins at the ready, though.'

After leaving Hap's Casey put his head down and his collar up and headed to Martha's as per Horn's instructions. Few people were out in the snow. Those who were had their eyes to the ground too and nobody even looked at him. He felt as alone as a ghost.

Martha was in the kitchen when he came in. She was stirring something on the stove. The room was warm and the cooking smelled good. She turned and looked at him and he knew right away that she'd heard the rumours too. Her mouth was straight and her eyes were angry. Before she could say a word he raised his hands to chest-height, palms outwards.

'I didn't do it, Martha,' he said. 'Whatever anyone's said it wasn't me.'

'I should ask you to leave,' she said.

He didn't want to go. The house was warm and the food smelt wonderful. Nevertheless he made the offer.

'I will if you want me to, Martha. But I want you to know I didn't do anything. If you don't believe me ask Hap, ask Marshal Horn.'

'You've spoken to the marshal?'

'We had a long chat. He wanted to lock me up.' Her eyes widened. 'For my own safety,' he added. 'Not because I'd done anything.'

'They say you were the last man to see Suzie.'

He could still sense uncertainty in her voice.

'Martha, I never killed her. But I did talk to her and I believe it was because of that that she was murdered. So I guess in a way I am to blame. It doesn't feel good.'

She stared at him for a few seconds longer. The anger in her eyes softened and for a few seconds she seemed to be focusing inwards. Maybe she was working back along the same line of logic that Hap had – that she was partly to blame for mentioning Suzie in the first place.

'You look cold,' she said eventually. 'Sit down. I've just been making up some stew. Coffee?'

'Please.' He sat down, and with fingers still trembling from the cold he dug out his paper and tobacco and started rolling a cigarette. She put a cup of coffee in front of him, then dished him up a huge plate of stew.

'Once you've warmed up you can tell me all about it,' she said.

That had been earlier. He had told Martha enough to keep her happy without mentioning any names or suspicions. He'd only been there a day but was already aware of how much she liked to gossip. Then he'd gone to bed early, wearing his silk long johns and a button down shirt against the cold. He was tired out from the emotions of the day but he lay there wide awake, shivering, and trying to slow his mind down. One moment his father was there, riding slowly down the trail towards the rock-fall, a woman who wasn't his wife on his mind, totally oblivious to the fact that death lay prone on the huge slab of rock ahead of him. The next moment it was Sam whom Casey pictured, the way she smiled and the way it felt when she touched him and looked at him. There was a connection there that he'd never felt before. He couldn't wait to see her again, but he was scared. Scared that he might be reading things into their few hours together that weren't really there; scared that it might turn out that there was already a man on the scene and she was only being friendly on account of their past; scared that it would turn out perfectly until he had to put a bullet in her brother. Now his mind conjured up Suzie, one moment lying there in front of him, shivering in her bed, a puzzled look on her face as she wondered why he wasn't getting undressed too, and the next moment in a coffin at Hap's, her throat sawn open and her skin cold. Now he was seeing the look in Milton's eyes as Milton realized that Casey was about to climb the stairs in Sloppy's and talk to Suzie, Milton calling to Suzie: *Don't say anything, Suzie. You know what I mean.* Milton waiting across the street for Casey to come out of the marshal's office, looking worried and nervous, demanding to know why Casey had been there. All of these thoughts spinning round and round in his head, keeping him awake and restless. When he did eventually fall asleep it was into an uneasy dream where the marshal was locking him into a cage and telling him he'd had his chance, the last train had come and gone and now they'd be waiting on the circuit judge.

Sometime in the small hours Casey was woken by the sound of a window being slid open and a freezing blast of cold air rushing into the room. He opened his eyes, ears straining, hairs on the back of his neck upright. Suddenly a black shape arose in front of him and Casey fumbled for the gun in his holster beneath his bed. But he was too slow. Something hard hit him on the side of the head and this time the unconsciousness that took him was dark and dreamless.

CHAPTER SIX

He woke up freezing. On a horse. Hands tied together behind so tightly he could barely feel them. As his senses returned so he gradually became more and more aware of his situation. He found he couldn't raise his hands and realized that not only were his hands bound together but he was also tied to the saddle. Then he realized that it wasn't the rope knotted round his wrists and stopping the blood that numbed his hands – it was the temperature. His feet were freezing too, so cold it felt like they finished at his ankles. He looked down, his vision wavered for a moment and he felt sick. As things came back into focus he saw his feet were bootless. And now that he had become aware of it he felt the cold cutting through his coat too. The coat hadn't been buttoned properly and he assumed that underneath he was only wearing the clothes he had gone to bed in. They must have thrown the coat over him but not worried about anything else.

There were four of them. They wore heavy coats and gloves, hats pulled low and bandannas knotted over the lower halves of their faces but they may as well have worn name tags. Their body language and voices told him who they were. The moon was almost full and cast more than enough light for him to realize where he was, and the desperateness of his situation.

Jagged Creek lay before him, frozen. The water looked

like a mirror painted on the white ground. The horse's hoofs crackled on the frozen ground. It was no longer snowing – it felt too cold for that – and the wind had dropped, but the clear sky meant that the ground, even here where it was usually soft and muddy, was as hard as rock. Ahead of him a cottonwood rose up against the skyline, its silhouette full of natural living lines and a single man-made one: a noose hanging still in the night. That was why they had taken the time to wrap a coat around him. They hadn't wanted him to freeze to death. Something else was planned.

They were laughing and giggling, wheeling their horses around him. They sounded drunk. One of them, Hudson, led the horse that Casey was on up towards the tree.

'Remember this?' Hudson said. 'Boy, you were as scared as a little girl.' Casey realized that the bandanna masks weren't to hide Hudson and the others from him, they were just in case anyone else came along and the boys had to ride away in a hurry. They might be seen but at least they wouldn't be recognized.

Casey twisted around in the saddle, looking for help from any quarter. At night the town was invisible from here, its buildings too low to be seen against the backdrop of mountains. There were no lights anywhere. No one awake. And even if there had been no one would be able to see them down here in the dark dip where the creek ran. He felt panic rising in his chest. His head ached where they had hit him and the more his consciousness returned the worse the pain. He tried to breathe deeply and slowly, but filling his lungs only pulled on his bound arms and made the panic rise higher.

'You won't get away with this,' he said. His voice came out quieter than he would have liked. It seemed to echo inside his aching head like a rock tumbling into a ravine.

Campbell was suddenly alongside him.

'But we will, Casey. See, most of the folk in town think that you killed that poor girl. And if they wake up in the morning to find that someone has lynched the killer, well, they'll probably not say so out loud, but inside they'll be mighty happy.'

'Marshal Horn knows I didn't kill her.'

'Marshal Horn is old and slow, Casey. He'll just be happy that another problem's been solved.'

They were almost beneath the cottonwood now. The thick branches of the tree obscured the moon.

'You cried last time,' Milton said. He spat on the ground and added, 'Yellow.'

Casey closed his eyes, breathed slowly, and determined to show no fear. His fingers – just a few moments ago numb – had started to hurt. He tried to ignore the pain.

'Only person I can recall crying is you, Milton,' he said. 'I seem to remember you were afraid of the dark. Fact I'm surprised you're out here now.'

'I ain't afraid of nothing, Yellow,' he said, but Casey knew he had touched a nerve.

'Wasn't it ghosts – Indian spirits you were scared of? Scared you were going to get scalped by a dead Indian?'

'Shut up, Yellow.'

'You should save your breath, Casey,' John Stark said. He was a little further away from Casey than the others, his horse a grey shape against the darker form of the mountains beyond.

Then they were under the tree and Campbell was leaning across and holding Casey tightly as Hudson reached up and brought the noose down. Casey tried to sway backwards out of the way but Campbell held him firm as Hudson threaded the rope over his head and pulled it tight. Then Campbell pulled a knife from a sheath, leaned over and sawed through the rope that held Casey's bound hands to the saddle. He was still tied at the wrists, but now

63

there was nothing holding him on the horse except his own balance.

They started laughing then, all of them. Wheeling their horses in circles and yee-ha-ing quietly. There was the sound of a bottle being opened and when the cork popped the horse stirred beneath him. Casey squeezed his legs together and whispered 'Whoah boy.'

'Been nice knowing you, Yellow,' Milton said. 'Good of you to come back and see us.'

'Imagine that,' Campbell said. 'Your daddy and now you. Seems that this town wasn't right lucky for the Angelos.'

Casey ignored them and tried to sit as still as possible. He gripped the horse lightly with his knees. *Please don't move*, he said almost to himself, his lips hardly moving. Inside the fear was rising higher and higher. He knew he couldn't panic – that was what they wanted – and he was determined not to give the boys any satisfaction at all. But the fear was crawling up his spine like something cold and alive. Out of nowhere a gentle breeze rolled across the plain and it felt like a frozen knife slicing into him as it riffled his meagre clothes and whispered through the horse's mane. He shivered. He shuddered. He couldn't recall ever having been so cold in his life but still couldn't be sure whether the shivers were because he was freezing or because he was frightened.

'You sitting comfortable, Yellow?' Milton asked.

'I'm fine.' The horse stirred again and the rope lifted his chin slightly. He tried to use the pressure of his knees to keep the horse steady. There was an imperceptible straining between him and the animal for a second and then the horse relaxed. This time at least.

'There's a long old while until dawn,' Hudson said. 'It's going to get colder, too.'

'Reckon the wind might get up some,' Campbell said.

'And that horse ain't going to want to stand up all night,' Hudson said.

'That horse ain't going to be *able* to stand up all night,' Milton added, and laughed.

'Why don't you just get it over with,' Casey said. The only way he could talk and not give away any sign of terror was through gritted teeth. The pain in his head was forgotten. The fear was everything. His whole world had closed in around him like a dark shroud; like a coffin lid being slid over him. Yet somehow, amidst all this fear, there was an image at the back of his mind, an image that made everything even worse. It was his mother standing on the porch with fresh tear-tracks on her cheeks and her skin white and drawn. It had been a terrible day when they'd heard the news about Robert Angelo. Until that moment Casey's parents had been so happy, so much in love. Like everyone they'd gone through their hard times but right then life was wonderful. The business was doing well. Casey was growing up into a fine man whom they could be proud of. They had good friends, a comfortable house, a future that they both looked forward to.

And then, out of the blue, the news about his father had arrived and, like a twister, had wiped everything away.

'Bring him home to me, Casey,' she had sobbed the previous morning. 'But please, be careful.' And he saw her now and knew it was an image of the way she'd be after receiving the news about his lynching.

'No point in rushing,' Hudson said, his bandanna lowered now to make the whiskey-drinking easier. He held up the bottle. 'Here's to old friendships.'

Casey hadn't begged the first time they had done this all those years ago – even though he had been scared for his life. Maybe somewhere deep inside he hadn't really believed them capable of such a thing, though afterwards he had always maintained that it had been for real. This time, though, there was no doubting what they were capable of. His father was dead. Suzie Cobb was dead. He was next and he was helpless to do anything about it. But still he refused to plead or to show them the fear that they so longed to see, the fear that was crushing his intestines with a vicelike grip, forcing a bad taste into his mouth and trembles into his legs.

'Old friends,' John Stark said.

'Old yellow friends.'

'Old friends.'

The men passed the whiskey around. They rode close to him and his horse fidgeted. They backed away, laughing. He found that it took all his attention to grip the horse with his knees, and he desperately tried to send it mental signals to hold still, to relax. He spoke quietly to it, not wanting to frighten it, not wanting to give any impression to Hudson and the others of how scared he was.

'You want some redeye, too, Casey?' Hudson asked.

Casey didn't answer.

'He's too busy trying to stay in the saddle,' Milton said.

'I think it might warm you up.' Hudson said.

'I'm OK,' Casey said. Warmth would be nice, heavenly even, but it wasn't his prime concern right now.

'I insist,' Hudson said, and rode up to Casey. 'Open up.'

'The way you're drawing this out anybody would think you're scared to kill a man,' Casey said.

Hudson smiled. 'I ain't scared of nothing. Now open up.'

Casey kept his mouth closed. Whiskey and cold weather and trying to keep balanced on a horse didn't go together. Casey realized that Hudson was thinking exactly the same thing.

'Campbell,' Hudson said. 'You care to pull on this rope a little?'

'My pleasure.'

Now Campbell rode over and there was his horse one side and Hudson's on the other. Campbell reached across, grabbed hold of the rope just above Casey's head and pulled upwards. He only had to exert a little pressure and suddenly Casey felt the noose tightening around his throat. He tilted his head backwards trying to go with the pull, trying to keep his throat open. He breathed through his nose determined to keep his mouth closed but when Hudson reached over and pinched Casey's nostrils he couldn't help but open his mouth. Immediately Hudson poured a good amount of whiskey in. Casey coughed and retched and his horse whinnied and fidgeted. Campbell reached across and steadied it and as Casey struggled for breath Hudson tipped more alcohol into his mouth. It was impossible to struggle too violently without frightening the horse. Casey spat as much of the rotgut out as he could but he swallowed more than he wanted to. The thing was, Hudson had been right. It did warm him. It burned as it went down and then the heat spread out from him in waves.

'I think he likes it,' Milton said, just as Casey spat the last mouthful out over Hudson. With that Hudson seemed to realize it was a good idea gone bad and probably a waste of good whiskey too, so he and Campbell moved away. They whispered something to one another, laughed a little, drank a little. They passed the bottle to Milton. Then to John Stark. Eventually they turned their attention back to Casey.

'We're going to leave you now, Casey,' Hudson said. 'Don't go away, huh?'

'He ain't going anywhere,' Campbell said. 'He'll just be hanging around.'

'Have fun, Yellow,' Milton said.

'We'll be back before sun-up,' Hudson said. 'Just to say hello, like.'

For a moment Casey thought they were joking. He had been convinced that at any moment one of them was going to ride up behind the horse he was on and give it a hard slap on the rump. A few steps forward and Casey would have been twisting in the wind. He didn't know whether this latest development was good or not. At least if they left they wouldn't see him die. That was something. And there was just a chance – a very slim chance – that if he could keep his balance and whisper to the horse all night long, maybe, just maybe, he could make it through to dawn. But then all that would mean would be he'd still be there when they returned.

'Just one final thing, Casey,' Hudson said. 'Milton.'

Milton rode closer then swung down off his horse. Casey saw the silver of a knife blade flash in the moonlight. For a moment he thought Milton was going to cut the horse, maybe kill it, maybe spook it. Either way Casey would be dead, and his heart hammered inside his chest and the taste of fear rose up into his throat. Then Campbell brought his horse over next to Casey's once more, reached out and caught hold of the reins that hung loose over Casey's horse's mane. 'We don't want her getting away from you, do we?' he said, and grinned, his teeth uneven and discoloured.

Casey was still convinced that he was going to die any moment. Yet somehow he still managed to speak.

'Tell me,' he said, his voice surprising him with its steadiness. 'For my own peace of mind. Which one of you bastards shot my father?'

Milton, still standing on the ground beside him, looked up. The moonlight cast shadows either side of his nose, giving him even more of a rodent-like countenance than normal. He smiled.

'You know, your daddy was—'

'We don't know nothing about that,' John Stark said

68

quickly. 'Do we, Milton?'

Both Casey and Milton looked across at Stark. His face was in shadow from his hat. His mouth was set straight.

There was a long pause.

'I guess not,' Milton said. He swung back up on his horse.

Casey was about to press the point further when his saddle suddenly slipped an inch to the left and he had to compensate by leaning slightly to the right. Instantly his blood ran cold, the taste of bile and the burn of whiskey rose in his mouth, and his hands started to shake. All thoughts about murder left his mind as he struggled to stay alive for even a few seconds longer. As Hudson and his gang rode away into the night, the sound of their laughter carrying a long way on the chill breeze, Casey tried to sit as still as a stone statue. Milton had cut through the saddle straps and any movement at all – from him or the horse – would almost certainly result in the saddle slipping off the side of the horse.

And Casey with it.

CHAPTER SEVEN

On the night when her brother was lynching Casey
Angelo, Samantha Ranier couldn't sleep. It wasn't a bad
insomnia, as it had been so many times before. Those had
been lonely sleepless nights, nights thinking of the father
she had once had, trying (and failing) to conjure his
image from the fading memories, trying to balance a love
that she knew she had once felt for him with the reality
that her father had been an evil and dangerous man,
trying to come to terms with being the daughter of a
murderer. It wasn't just her father, though. As the months
passed her mother had often been at the front of Sam's
mind as she lay there in the darkness. She often wondered
what her mother was thinking. How was she dealing with
those very same issues that kept Sam awake? Maybe they
ought to have shared their feelings more? But it had been
a subject that was barred from discussion in the Ranier
ranch.

'I don't want to talk about it,' her mother had said, her
mouth set in a hard straight line. 'Now or ever.'

And that was that. Years later Sam had often lain awake
wondering why her mother had remarried. No, that wasn't
strictly correct. Remarrying was understandable. A ranch
such as this needed a man around to run it. At the time
Hudson had been too young. No, that was wrong as well.
He hadn't been too young. He could have taken it on.

70

Together they'd all have got by somehow. But Hudson had shown no inclination for the hard work involved. Even now it was like trying to get blood out of stone getting him to do ranch work. So her mother had understandably remarried. But why to *him*? Why Henry Young of all people? Her mother was beautiful – especially then, ten years ago. Beautiful and rich. It wouldn't have been an exaggeration to say that she could have had any man in Tyburn Ridge or even the surrounding counties. Yet she'd plumped for a sour-faced bad-tempered man. Oh, Henry could be charming for sure – and maybe that was how it had happened. But he had an eye for the ladies, too. All that charm needed an outlet. Sam had even caught him looking at *her* once or twice when she had been preparing for a bath. She hadn't dared tell her mother. Just like she hadn't dared tell Violet the rumours she'd heard in town about Henry and the girls at Sloppy's.

In a way it was this second marriage of her mother's that was directly responsible for Sam's still being single. Seeing what had happened to her mother – what her mother had become – as a result of marrying Henry Young had made Sam absolutely determined to not marry just anyone. It would be the right man or no man at all. She'd told her mother this. And her brother. Hudson had laughed. He told her that it wouldn't last long, that pretty soon she'd be settling down with a local cowpoke and a growing belly. He'd even tried to persuade her to step out with Milton Craig. Milton Craig! That small weasel-faced man was exactly the type she was shying away from. She told Hudson this and he'd said how about Campbell James then? Campbell was only slightly better. A well built man, sure, and one not afraid of hard work. But still not marrying material. Those boys were more likely to end up in the jailhouse than on a cattle-drive.

Her mother hadn't tried to matchmake the way her

brother had, though she'd never given up entirely and had often raised the subject. 'You'll meet someone,' she insisted. 'You just watch.'

And this was precisely why Sam couldn't get to sleep.

So it was a nice insomnia for a change. She'd gone to bed early on account of it was so cold. Now she was lying there in the darkness with an almost full moon shining through her thin curtains, casting shadows in the middle of the night, giving everything an enchanted feel. When she closed her eyes she could see him. It was totally the opposite of what happened when she tried to conjure up her father. She found that Casey Angelo came to her easily: Casey in the stables haggling over a horse; Casey on the snow bound trail talking to her, trying hard to be charming and not say the wrong thing – and sometimes doing both simultaneously; Casey climbing the frozen rocks determined to figure out where his father's killer had lain; even the seventeen-year-old image of a young Casey naked in the creek appeared clear in her mind. It wasn't just pictures either. Lying there with her eyes closed and the blanket warming her she could sense everything about him as if he was just an arm's length away. Casey the boyish charmer. Casey the hero. Casey the child. Casey with his smooth dark skin and thick black hair and the bruised face that strangely neither he nor she had mentioned, though later her mother had told her of rumours about Hudson's brawl with the stranger in town. So Casey was a fighter, too. A fighter with bright and intense eyes, strong bones. He had grown tall and he carried himself with a confidence that made him appear larger still. His voice was soft but she sensed a tough side to him. He moved slowly but surely, like a cougar, and like a mountain lion he gave the impression of alertness and of possessing a coiled energy. There was even an aura of danger about him.

Yet even as she lay there enjoying the moonlight and the thoughts of Casey she still found herself struggling to keep these good thoughts uppermost in her mind. For not too far down there were less good thoughts. Thoughts she had no desire to dwell on. What would her mother and brother say if she told them how she felt about the son of the man who had brought their husband and father to the gallows? And what of Casey himself? She knew so little about him. She didn't believe that there was another woman in his life – after all, it had been Casey who had asked her if they could meet again. But then she thought of Henry Young and the girls at Sloppy's. Being married hadn't stopped Henry, had it? And though she sensed that Casey was cut from a very different cloth from Henry Young she didn't know this for sure. And then there was the fact that he would be leaving any day. Sure he'd said he could return – and when he'd said it she'd felt a warmth radiating out from her heart like she'd never experienced before – but did he really mean it? Would he mean it once he had returned home? She even had to ask herself if *she* had really meant it, if she really believed in these feelings? He was a handsome stranger on a quest and she was of an age that her mother had told her would see her resolve for independence weakening. Maybe it wasn't what she thought it was. Maybe it was just the excitement. But no, she refused to accept that. Casey had made her feel like no one had ever done before, and if that could happen in just a few hours was that not proof enough that the feelings were real?

There was another dark thought, too. One that had no form. One that sat at some lower level of her consciousness like a piece of bad news that you've temporarily forgotten but which you know is there. Someone had killed Casey's father and she knew, without admitting it to herself, that the reasons might be closer to home than she cared to contemplate.

So she pushed these thoughts away and concentrated on the good ones, the ones where they touched hands and it felt as though she'd brushed up against a hot stove. The ones where he spoke and made her laugh whatever he said. The ones where his smile made her heart beat faster and where his determination made her want to help him, to be there for him, to be by his side. And in the darkness she smiled, blissfully unaware that shortly the dark thoughts would take over and crystallize in front of her, and that the romantic moon would illuminate terrors, not passions.

Casey realized immediately that the belief that if he could remain still enough for long enough then he might just survive until dawn was wrong. The cold was eating into him like snake poison slipping through his veins. He knew that he would freeze to death if he didn't move. And if he moved he would hang. For the moment he sat as still as possible. He tried to work his hands free but the knots were too tight and his fingers too numb. He forced himself to breathe slowly and try to ignore the bitter cold. He had no idea what time it was but the moon looked to be on its descent – though only just. Below him he could feel the horse shivering. He squeezed his legs together to give the animal some comfort and to let the horse know that he wasn't alone. The animal shifted slightly below him. 'Steady,' Casey said, his voice little more than a whisper. He was sure they were watching him. To start with he couldn't understand why they hadn't just killed him. But now he realized that *this* way was so much more cruel. He was shivering and shaking and his insides were knotted with fear. It was almost *too* cruel. The tree rose above him like a dark skeletal creature waiting to pluck his life away. The moonlight created black and white and silver patterns on the frozen ground so beautiful that it just added more pain and regret for the world that he would be leaving any moment. They had known exactly what they were doing. They had probably stored up the idea for ten years, waiting for an opportunity such as this. They were crueller than he'd ever imagined. And thus he was sure they were watching. But when his eyes roved the landscape he saw no movement, heard no sound. There was nothing out of place. They had said they would return before dawn. Maybe they weren't watching then. Maybe they'd just come back for the horse and watch him swing for a few minutes. He flexed his fingers and tried the knots again.

Nothing.

Now that he was alone – and despite the fear that had enveloped him and his impending certain death – he found himself thinking about what had just happened. Milton had been about to say something. And maybe if Casey had have pushed him – or them – harder they would have boasted about the killing. After all, there was no reason not to. They had nothing to lose and would have probably enjoyed the gloating. But then John Stark had cut the conversation dead.

The horse moved forwards beneath him.

'Whoah boy!' Casey said softly. The horse was getting edgy. Casey could feel the animal's shivers growing in intensity. Now the horse raised a hoof and with the movement Casey felt himself slipping. He squeezed his legs together and twisted to stay upright. A few years previously, a Portuguese acrobatic troop had come through Omaha on their way West. They had performed amazing stunts, contorting themselves into strange positions and balancing on top of each other's hands and feet. Afterwards Casey had asked one of the men how they did it.

'It's easy,' the man had told him. 'The person on top,

75

he stay still, as still as possible. The person below he do all the work. You want to try?' Casey had laughed and had politely refused the offer but the man's words came back to him now. *The person below he do all the work.* And now, in order to stay alive, Casey was having to do precisely the opposite. The horse moved and he tried to compensate. And all the time the cold was seeping into their bones making concentration ever more difficult.

'Stay still,' Casey said, louder now, and the words frosted in the air in front of his face. It was no use, he couldn't even stay still himself. He was beyond shivering, beyond shaking, even. He had the shudders and with every violent one of them he fully expected the saddle to slide off the horse and take him into a cold eternal darkness. Still he tried to work the knots holding his wrists fast but his fingers felt three times their normal size. The horse moved again. He was getting restless. It was just a matter of time before he would simply give up and pull away, seeking shelter and warmth, and it could only have been years of conditioning that had kept him there even this long. Casey guessed that as soon as he was too cold to squeeze the horse's flanks any longer the animal would simply wander off. Even if the horse simply lowered himself gently to the floor seeking his own warmth against the ground Casey would die. Casey knew then that this was it. The sky was clear, not a cloud to obscure the dark blue eternity. It went on for ever. Looking up there made him dizzy and he felt tears in his eyes. The moon cast long shadows, almost like the sun. Casey could see the stars. Millions of stars. Even as his vision blurred everything was being imprinted on his memory for the last time. He breathed out huge clouds of freezing moisture, not crying aloud, but sobbing inside for his mother and his father and all the days he would never see. He wasn't scared of dying, but he was fearful of the pain his death would cause and of the unfinished business he would leave. Now his lips and nose were stiff with ice. His muscles were too cold. He closed his eyes and in the darkness he heard the horse cough and snort and then move again.

This time Casey over-corrected and the saddle slipped further. He tried to squeeze his knees together and for a moment he thought he'd saved himself for a few more minutes. But then gravity caught the heavy leather saddle and everything went light.

Casey managed one deep breath before the rope closed around his neck.

There was something wrong. Sam didn't know how she knew this but she knew it was true. She had come to with a start and felt as scared as if it had been a terrible dream that had brought her awake. But it wasn't a dream that had woken her – it was the sound of the boys outside, laughing, whispering drunkenly, telling each other to shush, it was the sound of snorting horses and the pop of a cork. It was the ratchet of a revolver's cylinder being spun.

She pulled back the covers and, shivering, moved the thin curtain aside and peered out. The moon illuminated her brother and Milton Craig and Campbell James sitting on their horses looking down at John Stark. Hudson was passing a bottle to Milton. Campbell was the one spinning his revolver. John Stark was kneeling on the white ground, gloves on the floor next to him. He was looping a long thick piece of rope into a hangman's noose.

She let the curtain fall back until there was just the narrowest of gaps to peer through. Her heart was racing. She'd thought about the fight in Sloppy's that her mother had told her about. Casey was bruised but he didn't seem injured otherwise. He hadn't mentioned it. Now she wondered if it had been four on to one and that the others were embarrassed. Maybe Casey had shown them up. She'd sensed an anger in them that afternoon even prior to knowing about the brawl. And they'd never liked Casey when he had been a kid anyway. They had liked him a lot less after his father had brought Spencer Ranier to justice. Anger had been festering inside them for ten years now.

She had no doubt that the noose they were fashioning was being made with Casey Angelo in mind.

She pulled on thick trousers over the silk leggings she'd been wearing to keep warm, then a thick shirt, boots, a scarf, her coat, hat, and lastly gloves. She snatched another look out of the window. The boys were just riding out in the direction of town. She closed her bedroom door and made her way as quietly as she could outside.

In the stable she rushed to saddle up her mare, aware that with every second her brother and his cronies were getting closer to town. After what seemed an age of fumbling with cold fingers on leather she had the saddle tied down, the bit in the horse's mouth and the reins to hand. She led the horse out into the freezing night and had just mounted the horse when Henry Young stepped out of the darkness, the moon reflecting off his face as he adjusted his hat and reached up to grab her reins.

'It's a bit late to be riding out, Sam? Where ya'll going.'

She looked down at him, heart racing with anxiety to be on her way.

'I go where I like,' she said.

'Not at this time of night.' His eyes were moon-shadowed under the brim of his hat but she could see the line of his thin sneering lips.

'What does that mean?'

'It means I have a duty to protect you.'

'What?'

'Whilst you're living under this roof and you ain't got any other man to look after you then you're my responsibility. So best you turn right around.'

She jerked the mare's head to the left trying to pull the reins from Henry's grasp, but he held tight.

'Ain't no good arguing,' he said. 'You be a good girl and do as you're told.'

'I'm going.'

'Only place you're going is back inside.'

'No.' She couldn't resist looking away from him and down the trail. There was no sign of the other riders.

'They're long gone,' he said.

'Why didn't you stop them?'

'They can look after themselves.'

'So can I.'

'You were going to follow them.' It wasn't a question. It was a statement. Maybe it was the answer to the question she hadn't asked: *why are you trying to stop me?*

'Do you know where they've gone?' she asked.

'Can't say I do.' She couldn't see his eyes and thus had no clue as to whether he was lying or not.

'Did you see them before they left?' she said.

Now he paused.

'You *did* see them, didn't you?' she said. 'You saw what they were doing! What they were making.'

'I was awake,' he said. 'I *heard* them, is all. Now I think it's best you come back inside and leave the boys to do whatever it is that they're doing.'

'You can't just let them . . .'

'Let them what?'

She said nothing. She didn't want to voice her fears. That might make them even more real.

'A girl was killed yesterday, Sam.'

'What?'

'I said a girl was killed.'

'Killed? Who?' Despite her anxiety to get away he now had at least a little bit of her attention.

'A girl by the name of Suzie Cobb.'

She shook her head. She didn't know the girl.

'They're going after the killer,' he said.

For a moment everything seemed to slow down, the urgency to be riding after her brother dulled. If they were going after Suzie's killer then they weren't going after Casey. And no matter how terrible it was that someone was likely to get lynched she couldn't help but feel a tiny relief in her heart.

'She worked at Sloppy's,' he said.

And now it fell into place – the reason he hadn't stopped the boys. Suzie Cobb was probably one of Henry's favourites. And that brought back the distaste that was always near whenever she spoke to Henry. Was Suzie one of the ones he had cheated on her mother with?

He saw the look on her face. 'They're good girls, Samantha.'

'Good girls? *Good* girls? You think maybe I could get a job there?'

'Don't get funny with me.' He shivered. 'Now come inside.'

'What happened? Who told you about it?'

'It's the talk of the town.'

'What happened?'

'It was that Casey Angelo. He cut her throat.'

Everything wavered in front of her. It was like the instance when branding-smoke hit the eyes and blurred the vision. One second she had begin to relax and now . . . now it turned out that it *was* Casey they were after. But not just because of the antagonism that had arisen between him and the boys over a fight, now it was over a murder.

'No!' she said.

'Oh, yes. If you hadn't eaten supper alone and slipped off to bed so early you'd have heard all about it too.'

Her horse snorted and jerked his head. She wasn't sure

if it was because of the freezing temperature or because the horse was picking up on her anger and desperation.

'Apparently he went up to see her last night,' Henry said. 'Guess he wasn't prepared to pay because he cut her throat and left her lying there in bed. Nice boy, this Casey. You want my opinion he deserves everything he gets. Now you put that horse away and come back . . .'

She pulled the reins hard left, the horse went with her and Henry stumbled but still tried to hold on to the leather. As he looked up at her, anger and victory on his face, she kicked out and the point of her boot caught him square on the chin. He dropped the reins and fell to his knees. Instantly she urged the horse forward, galloping into the night.

She rode as fast as she dared in the freezing darkness. If Casey was accused of murder – and she knew it could only be an accusation, for he would never have done such a thing, not the Casey she had met yesterday and not the Casey she had known fifteen years ago – then he'd be at the jailhouse. There was no way to get anyone out of the jailhouse unless you had the keys or were prepared to blow up the side of the building with some mining dynamite. She couldn't imagine her brother and his friends setting out to do that. None of them knew the first thing about dynamite and they'd probably end up killing everyone inside the jail. Then again, maybe Casey was the only person in the jail, in which case they might see that as good a plan as any. But it was more likely that somehow they had got hold of the keys and were going to unlock him and then . . . She shuddered as a vivid picture of John Stark knotting that rope into a noose came into her mind. She wondered if anyone else from Tyburn Ridge was in on it. Maybe the marshal? But surely not; Marshal Horn took his job far too seriously to get involved in anything as outside the law as a lynching. Though yesterday on the ride out to the place where his father had been murdered Casey had mentioned that he'd already riled Marshal Horn slightly. But no, that wasn't reason enough for a lawman to be in on a lynching. It was more likely they'd stolen the keys when Horn was out or distracted. Even that didn't sound feasible but whatever plan they had in mind she couldn't bear to consider the ending so she urged the horse forward over the hard, frozen ground, praying that it didn't lose its footing in a hole or a frozen puddle. At least the moon gave plenty of illumination.

There was no sign of the boys ahead of her. She pushed the horse harder, felt her own shoulder-blades grow damp with the effort and concentration. In the summer a dust cloud would have given her a clue as to how far ahead they were. In the frozen night there was nothing.

She galloped around the twist in the road where Casey's father had been murdered. Such a terrible thing but at least it had brought Casey back to Tyburn Ridge. She didn't dwell on the fact of the murder too long. There were so many dark thoughts and ideas growing in her mind that she couldn't allow herself to delve too deeply. There would be time enough for that – and when it came she knew that it was not going to be good.

Eventually ahead of her she saw the dark hollow where, in daylight, the buildings of Tyburn Ridge would be visible. For now they were shrouded by the night. She slowed, still feeling a desperate urgency, but needing to catch her breath, needing to make a plan. But instead of a plan forming it was a feeling of futility that swept over her. What could she do? One girl against four determined men – maybe more than four. They appeared to have Henry's blessing so it followed that maybe they'd had the support of many of the townsfolk, too. Casey had already fought with her brother in public, riled the marshal, and – in the townsfolk's eyes at least – had killed the girl from Sloppy's.

Sitting there on the mare, with the moon casting her motionless shadow before her and the wind biting through her blanket-lined coat, she realized that there was nothing she could do. She hadn't even brought along a gun. She was about to curse her stupidity when she heard voices and the sound of horses' hoofs on the frozen ground ahead of her.

Quickly she turned and cast around for somewhere to hide. There were several trees and some thick sagebrush to her right. She moved the horse into the cover and waited, a hand gently stroking the mare's head, willing her to remain still and quiet.

They came past her at a steady pace but they weren't looking out for anyone and consequently they didn't glance her way. Four riders wearing bandannas as masks, but she knew who they were: her brother, Milton, Campbell and John Stark; and in-between Campbell and John Stark was someone thrown over a horse. Whoever it was looked asleep or unconscious. Or dead.

It had to be Casey. She felt it in her bones – a chill much colder and sharper than the night weather could create. She couldn't believe how quickly they had broken him out of jail. There were no noise or lights coming from the town. No one following them – either in support or chase. They hadn't been that far ahead of her. It seemed that they must have just ghosted into town, opened his cell door, and taken him out. And that scared her more than anything. For that suggested that the whole town was consenting.

They laughed as they rode, their voices growing louder as they pulled away from town. Someone asked if he was awake yet?

'Ain't stirring yet,' someone said, it sounded like Campbell.

'Hope you didn't hit him too hard. Wouldn't want to spoil the fun.'

'He's still breathing.'

'For the time being.'

'He's going to be right surprised when he wakes up.'

'We going to use the same tree as we did all them years ago, Hud?'

'Indeed we are.'

As their voices and shapes faded Sam realized what it was that they were talking about. She knew the story of how they'd pretended to hang Casey when he was just a boy. He'd told her and sworn her to secrecy. He hadn't wanted his father to know. They were taking him to the same place. To Jagged Creek. To the very same tree – one that he'd shown her years before. But this time, she realized, it was for real.

Sam knew these trails and gullies as well as any man. No sooner were they out of earshot than she wheeled the horse and galloped off in seemingly the opposite direction. It was a longer route. She would cross the creek at a shallow ford nearer town and come round at them from the far side, the mountains hiding her silhouette from a distance, the trees down there hiding her close up.

It would be tight, timewise, to get there before they did.

And she still didn't know what she was going to do when she arrived.

At the creek she stopped. She then eased the horse forward very slowly, trying to lead her into putting just one foot on the frozen water, before apply any weight. But the horse had picked up on her anxiety and seemed determined to pull against any hesitation. It stepped forward into the creek confidently and, she feared, too quickly. The ice held but suddenly she felt the horse slip a little. She gasped and her heart rose into her mouth. A broken foot now wouldn't just mean a long walk home for her. It would mean the end of Casey too. Now the ice crackled and finally broke. The horse snorted as its feet went down into the icy water and found solid ground below. Then they were across and galloping into the night, the creek to their left, the hanging tree far away – *too* far away, she thought – ahead of them.

By the time they got there Sam was convinced that they were too late. The ride had seemed to take for ever. But still she kept her wits about her. She slowed the horse knowing that the sound of its snorting and heaving would carry on the cold night air. Once she could hear their voices she stopped altogether, dismounted, whispered to her horse to stay still, and then edged as close as she could on foot.

When she saw what they were doing to him every instinct screamed for her to burst out into the open and try and save him. He was helpless. Conscious now, they had him sitting upright on the horse, his hands bound behind him, a noose over his head. She gasped and the sound seemed to roll across the frozen ground towards the men. But none of them noticed. They were drinking, laughing, talking. She watched them pour something – whiskey, presumably – down Casey's throat. At any moment, she thought they were going to slap the horse on the rump and it would bolt forward leaving Casey hanging. And she had absolutely no idea what she could do to stop it. All her muscles were tensed, she would have to race forward when it happened and . . . and what? Yet they never did frighten the horse into bolting. Instead, it seemed, they were teasing him, torturing him even, and slowly – listening to the conversation – she realized what they were doing. They were going to leave him. They were simply going to ride away and leave him balanced like that in the sub-zero temperature. It was as good as slapping the horse on the rump, only far more cruel. The horse would only have to move forward a yard – which sooner or later it would surely do – and Casey would be dead. Yet despite all of this she heard Casey asking them about his father, his voice strong and seemingly fearless, even on the brink of death he wanted to know the truth. She felt a rush of attraction for him so strong that for a moment her face burned despite the coldness in the air. She heard Milton start to say something and she heard John Stark cut him off. Then there was a moment's confusion when Milton climbed down off his horse and did something beneath Casey's mount. It only took a moment for the confusion to make sense – Milton had cut the saddle straps! Casey was balancing upon a cold and tired horse, his head in a noose, and the saddle was loose.

Then the boys rode off.

She waited as long as she dared. She couldn't break cover until she was sure they had gone. But maybe they would stop somewhere up ahead and wait, probably turn and watch. Yet once they were out of side the urge was irresistible. She stood up and immediately the horse Casey was on snorted and fidgeted.

'Whoah boy,' Casey said.

She stood very still. The horse settled. She realized she didn't even have a knife. How could she have been so foolish? Then again, she hadn't known what Hudson and the boys were going to do. Still, she should have brought something, some weapon.

Now she edged forward. Very slowly, not wanting to alarm the horse.

'Casey,' she whispered. Her voice seemed loud to her but he didn't hear. The horse shook itself.

She moved closer. The horse knew she was there. She was just about to whisper his name again or maybe say something to calm the horse when it moved again. This time it was too great a movement. Almost in slow motion she saw Casey lean one way, then the other, and finally slip off the horse, the rope around his neck tightening and pulling him upright.

'No!' she screamed. And raced forward.

The rope pulled tightly around his throat. Immediately he started choking. The breath he'd drawn as he slid slowly off the horse was now caught inside him, the air turning to poison as his body drew all of the goodness from it and was unable to expel what it didn't need, or pull in fresh good air. So this is how outlaws feel, he thought, the lack of oxygen starting to create a feeling of almost drunken elation inside him as he twisted in the freezing moonlight. He knew death was mere seconds away. It should have been instantaneous. Done right the fall itself would break a man's neck and deliver him straight to hell. But this time everything had happened in a slow and graceful manner. The horse had moved – spooked by something or possibly just too cold to stand still any longer – and the saddle had eased him slowly into thin air. So he'd suffocate instead of having his neck broken. It all added up to the same thing.

And then, as the light started to darken as if a cloud had scudded in front of the moon, he heard someone shout. A girl's voice. Now there were hands around his legs, his waist, pushing him upwards, lifting him, and just for a second the tightness around his throat eased, not by much, not enough to take a deep breath, but enough to let the bad air come whistling out and for him to take a wheezing breath of new air, to hang on to life for a few seconds longer.

'Casey!' she said. 'It's me! Sam.'

He wanted to look at her. He wanted to speak. He could do neither. The rope around his neck made any speech impossible and his eyes were closed, the pressure inside his head too great, too painful for him to do anything now.

'I can't hold you,' she said. There were tears in her voice. 'I can't hold you, Casey!'

Don't let me go, he thought. Not now. I was ready for

this a few moments ago. Now I'm not. Now there's a chance please don't let me go. He managed to grab another breath before her hands slipped and the rope tightened once more. Then she lifted him again but he knew it was futile. She couldn't hold him all night any more than the horse could have done.

The horse . . .

Maybe she read his mind for now he could hear her calling, whistling, and urging the horse back towards him. He managed to open his eyes just a slit. The pressure behind them felt as though they might burst. And he saw the horse wandering away, further away. He closed his eyes again. It hurt too much to keep them open.

Yet now there was something pressing against him, something big and strong. And she was urging him to help her. There *was* a horse. *Her* horse. She was wrestling with his legs, arguing with the horse, telling it to move, telling him to move. Everything was dark now but somehow she got the horse under him and now the pressure of his own weight was gone. But the rope was still too tight. There was no gap at all for air to get in or out of his lungs.

'Hold on, Casey,' she said. 'Just hold on.' And they were the last words he heard for a moment.

He could breathe.

His hands were still tied behind him and the rope was still around his neck – in fact he was back in just the position he had been a few minutes before – but at least he could breathe.

And then he could feel her fingers working at the noose, loosening it, letting that pure freezing air rush into his lungs. The sweetest taste of all his life, like cold mountain water on a hot summer's day, like the day he splashed naked with her in Jagged Creek. At last she had the noose loose enough. She told him to lean forward and she lifted it from his neck.

He was still alive.

It wasn't over yet.

CHAPTER EIGHT

They knocked quietly but persistently on Hap's door until he stumbled down the stairs and asked grumpily from behind the closed door who had died.

'No one,' Casey croaked, as the undertaker swung open the door. 'But it was close.'

The shoulders of Casey's coat were white with frost. His lips were blue and his eyebrows frozen. And his hands were still knotted behind him. Sam was in an equally sorry condition. Her fingers had become too cold to undo the knots around Casey's wrists, so, with the noose off, she had led him back to town. She hadn't known where to take him, but he'd suggested Hap's.

'I think he might be the only friend I've got left in town,' he'd said. 'Present company excepted, of course.'

'My goodness,' Hap said, stepping out into the freezing air, squinting without his spectacles on but recognizing trouble when he saw it. 'Who did this to you?'

'It was my brother,' Sam said. The words weren't as hard to say as she had expected them to be. Maybe later the implications would hit her.

Hap sighed. 'Come inside. Both of you. The stove is still warm.'

'I need to settle the horses,' Sam said.

'You're frozen,' Hap said. 'You come in. I'll take care of the horses.'

'It's OK. You take care of Casey. I'll look after the horses.'

'Round the back then,' Hap said. 'Straight down the alley at the side. There's shelter from the worst of it there and I have blankets and a little hay. I'll be out in a moment. Come on, Casey, let's get you inside where it's warm. My word, you haven't even got proper clothes on under that coat.'

Half an hour later things seemed a whole lot better. The horses were pressed up against each other in Hap's yard, sheltered from the wind, blanketed, and with plenty of hay to eat. Hap had cut the ropes from Casey's wrist with a silver scalpel and had wrapped him in a thick blanket. He'd made them all strong sweet coffee which was scorching hot and laced with good whiskey. Casey's hands still trembled uncontrollably and he felt as if his whole body was grown around a core of solid ice. His toes and fingers were agony as feeling returned to them – but it was a nice agony. It proved he was still alive. There were deep red marks around his throat where the noose had bit into him and his voice was as rough as tarpaper when he told Hap and Sam what had happened. After Sam had told it from her point of view Casey said:

'I'd love to be out there when they come back.'

'That'll be some expression they'll have on their faces,' Hap said.

'I can't believe it,' Sam said. 'My own brother.'

Casey frowned. 'Maybe you shouldn't be involved in this, Sam.'

She glared at him. 'What do you mean? I saved your life.'

He put his cup down and reached for her hands. They

were as cold as his own. 'I know. And I'll be forever grateful. But I don't want to hurt you. I don't want you to hate me.'

'I won't hate you.'

'They killed my father,' he said.

'You still have no proof, Casey,' Hap said.

'How much proof do you want? Why would they have tried to hang me tonight? They were trying to silence me, Hap.'

'A lot of people still think you're responsible for what happened to Suzie Cobb.'

Casey nodded. 'I know. That's why they did it this way. It would have looked like a lynching and in a week or two everybody would have forgotten all about it. They knew Suzie had talked to me. They knew I was asking too many questions. I even told Sully down at the stables that I'd found something along the trail where my father had been shot.'

'What?' Sam asked. 'What did you find?'

'I didn't find anything. I just made Sully believe that I had. I figured that he'd tell someone, the word would spread, and – I guess – I'd provoke a reaction.'

'It certainly worked.'

'A little too well.'

'But you still don't have a shred of evidence.'

Casey sipped the steaming coffee. He needed a cigarette but his fingers were too cold to roll one. 'I'll get evidence' he said. 'And if I don't – well, so be it.' Now he looked across at Sam. Her hair was damp where the frost had melted. Her cheeks were red and her eyes tired. She looked more beautiful than ever, more beautiful than the glimpse of the moon that he had thought was going to be the last thing he saw, more beautiful than the silver frost that had coated the ground upon which he thought he was going to die. 'I'm so scared I'm going to hurt you,' he whispered.

She blinked and two tears spilled over her eyelids. He reached across and brushed them away, his touch more clumsy than he'd meant.

'I'm sorry,' he said. 'I still can't feel my fingers.'

'It's OK.'

'No it's not. My father . . . my family and your family. Is this what our destiny holds? For another generation of each to hurt one another.'

'It's all right,' she said, but he knew it wasn't. Not yet. There was confusion and heartbreak brewing inside her and he was helpless to stop it. She had saved his life, but even before that he'd found it impossible to stop thinking about her. He'd been looking forward to seeing her again but hadn't for a moment imagined it would be under such circumstances. And now, frozen and still within spitting distance of death, he was already thinking ahead to the moment when he could exact his revenge.

By killing her brother.

Hap made more coffee. Casey managed at last to roll a cigarette. For a while they were quiet. Sam went out into the yard, ostensibly to check on the horses but both Casey and Hap understood that she needed to be alone.

'She's a beautiful girl,' Hap said.

Casey nodded.

'Her mother was once, too.'

Casey nodded again. 'I like her, Hap. I like her a lot. But I can't just walk away. I didn't come here just to collect my father's body and go home.'

'I know.'

'And I'm close now.'

'You still have to prove it, Casey. You can't go killing someone just because you're convinced inside. That'll make you as bad as them.'

'I'll find proof.'

When Sam came back in there were fresh tear tracks on her face. She wiped her cheeks with the back of her hand and managed to smile. Then, as if she'd overheard the conversation she said:

'Milton's the weak one. Milton's the one who was going to tell you something before John Stark stopped him.'

Casey looked at Hap and then back at Sam.

'You want proof then Milton's where you should concentrate,' she added.

They drank even more coffee laced with even more whiskey. Casey and Hap rolled and smoked more cigarettes. Slowly Casey and Sam thawed out. They threw ideas at one another. Somehow they laughed and wished they could see the faces of Hudson and the gang when they returned to the creek to find the empty noose hanging there, no sign of Casey or of the horse.

'They'll think they're seeing things,' Sam said, her voice tinged with hidden sadness as if she knew she had crossed a line that not many people ever had to step over but was trying to keep the pain secret from the men.

'Like a ghost,' Hap said. 'One moment you were there, the next – gone.'

Casey looked at Hap. Then across at Sam. There must have been something in his eyes for she asked:

'What is it, Casey?'

'*Like a ghost*,' he said.

'I don't understand.'

'Milton's scared of ghosts,' he said. 'I mentioned it tonight. I remembered he was scared of the dark when we were kids – Indian spirits, especially. He was always scared he was going to get scalped by a dead Indian. I thought he'd have grown out of it but I had no other way of fighting back earlier and I just said it. I didn't think it would mean anything but he snapped back at me like I'd touched a raw nerve.'

Hap shook his head, an admiring smile forming on his lips.

'What is it, Hap?' Casey asked.

'Nothing.'

'No, go on.'

'I was just thinking. You remind me of your pa, Casey. There you were about to be lynched, and you're still fighting back, albeit just with words.'

'Anybody would've done it.'

'No they wouldn't. Most people would have been too terrified to say anything but prayers.'

'He was asking them about his pa, too,' Sam said. 'I was listening. Even then he was still trying to find out what had happened.' She looked at him and smiled and Casey felt himself blushing.

'Let's get back to these ghosts,' Casey said.

'Ghosts,' Hap said.

'And Milton's scared of them,' Sam said.

'I think . . . I don't know, but I reckon if we can scare Milton enough – if we can get him alone, in the night, and scare him enough, then he'll tell us exactly what happened.'

'And you're going to scare him how?' Sam asked.

'With a ghost.'

'Any particular one? It's not going to be easy to conjure up a dead Indian.'

'Not an Indian,' Casey said.

'Who, then? You? Back from the dead?'

'Not me, either.'

Now Hap was nodding. He'd cottoned on to Casey's plan. He took off his spectacles as if preparing to make a great revelation.

'Your father,' he said.

'Yep, my father.'

'It could work,' Hap said. 'Though the first bit mightn't be so pleasant.'

'What are you men talking about?' Sam asked.

'He's going to dress up as his father,' Hap said. 'And go and see Milton.'

CHAPTER NINE

The next day was the longest day of Casey's life, or so it seemed. They had decided that it was best he hide for the entire day. They'd made a plan and Sam was to try and get Milton alone that night. What with the full moon and Robert Angelo rising up from the dead, they figured Milton might well crack and reveal something. It was certainly worth a shot. But meanwhile Casey had to stay hidden. The fact that he'd disappeared from the noose would only add to the spooky atmosphere they were hoping to scare Milton with. So Casey remained in Hap's house all day long. In itself, that wasn't so tough – the weather was still bad outside and Hap had the stove on and a good supply of coffee and whiskey – but it was the not knowing about how Sam was getting on that made it difficult. She'd told them both about how she'd kicked Henry Young on the chin as she'd raced after her brother and his gang the night before. She was going to have to go home and face Henry's wrath before being able to put any other part of their plan in place.

About mid-morning there was a hammering on Hap's door. Hap snuck a quick look through an upstairs window.

'It's the marshal.'

That made sense. Marshal Horn had told Casey he'd better be on the eastbound train that morning. They'd heard the train whistle about an hour previously, sounding distant yet clear through the cold atmosphere. Casey could imagine Horn waiting on the platform in his heavy coat and hat, cursing the weather and cursing Casey for not turning up. Then Horn would've trudged back into town and what was the betting that the first place he went would have been Martha's boarding-house?

And there was the first problem.

All of Casey's clothes – and his gun – were still over at Martha's. As far as he was concerned (and, he hoped, she too) he hadn't booked out. Come the morning, if all went according to plan, he'd go back over there for his gun and clothes. Meanwhile, he had borrowed a shirt, trousers, and some tight-fitting boots off Hap.

So here was Horn. Having been to Martha's and found him not there Horn was no doubt doing the rounds of likely haunts. And Hap's was an obvious choice, what with Casey's father being there.

'You're going to have to hide,' Hap said. 'I wouldn't put it past him to want to sniff around a little.'

'Where's a good place?'

'Here,' Hap said, pointing to a coffin on the floor.

'What?'

Horn was knocking on the door again, calling out Hap's name.

'No time to argue, Casey. In you get.'

Casey lay down in a coffin and Hap slid the lid across. It was pitch black and eerily cold inside considering the warmth in the room. Casey's breathing sounded awfully loud. He could even hear his own heart. He recalled the moment the previous night when the noose around his head and the freezing night and the fear of his impending death had all conspired to produce the claustrophobic feeling of a coffin lid closing upon him. Now he knew how it really felt. Another story came to mind: he'd heard tell one time of some soldiers down New Mexico way who'd nailed a live Apache scout into a coffin. The story went that they were going to leave him there all day long. They set the coffin down a fair ways from their camp so the Indian wouldn't be able to hear a thing and left him in the desert heat, figuring that by nightfall he'd be more than willing to tell them where the Apache camp was. Trouble was the main Apache party raided that afternoon and killed every single last one of the soldiers. He'd heard the story from a trapper who'd heard it from a cavalry officer who'd heard it from a buffalo-hunter. No one knew if it was true or not, and if it was who could have told it? – on account of all the soldiers were massacred by the Indians. But the way the story went, that Apache scout was still out there somewhere in a sealed box in the hot desert.

Casey thought of the story now as he tried to slow his breathing and still his pounding heart.

Then he heard Hap and Horn come into the room.

'No, I've not seen him since before yesterday,' Hap said.

'And his father's body is still here?'

'Yes. He's going to take him home.'

'I rather hoped he was going to be going home today.'

'I don't think he'd go without his father.'

'No, me neither. He's been nothing but trouble since he arrived.'

'Marshal?'

'Well, first he has a fight with Hudson Ranier and his boys. Riles 'em up bad. Then that Suzie Cobb gets murdered – and whilst I don't think Casey was the one that did it, I have no doubt that his presence is why it happened. He was out looking at the place where his father was shot and he told Sully down at the stables that he found something there.'

'What?'

'He didn't say. But Sully likes to tell everyone everything he knows so you can rest assured that whoever did kill

Casey's father is a little bit nervous right now.'

'And now Casey's disappeared?'

'Yep. Part of me is worried about him and part of me is angry.'

'Have you got a message for him, if he comes in?'

'Tell him to get on down to my office pretty darn quick. Or, better still, leave town even quicker.'

After Horn had left Hap slid the lid off the coffin. Casey wiped sweat from his brow. The cold interior of the coffin had warmed up like an oven with his body heat. He couldn't stop thinking about that Apache scout.

'He wasn't very happy,' Hap said.

'I heard.'

'He reckons you've got the killers nervous.'

'Just the way I like them.'

And so the hours dragged on. The cold wind howled along Main Street, bringing with it flurries of sleet and a darkness that was more dusk than midday. Sometime in the early afternoon there was another knock on Hap's door.

Hap took another peek out of the window.

'It's Hudson Ranier,' he said.

Sam knew that Henry Young would be waiting for her. But she had no idea of what he would say or do. He'd never laid a hand in her in anger before – but there was always a first time, and maybe her kicking him square on the chin might be just the trigger that he needed. She also knew that he, like most of the cowboys, was an early riser. He'd be up with the sun. So she'd left Hap's an hour before dawn, hoping to get home too early for Henry to have risen.

She was tired beyond belief, both physically and mentally. She had been running on nerves and coffee all night long. And now that she had got cold all over again she just wanted to curl up in her bed and sleep until midday. After that she had to somehow find Milton and persuade him to go walking with her that evening. She had told Casey and Hap that it wouldn't be a problem, that Milton still asked her more or less every month to step out with him. This wasn't strictly true. After she'd told Hudson how she felt about him Milton had avoided her altogether. Still, she was pretty sure she could get him alone.

'It'll need to be somewhere warm,' Hap had said. 'This is no weather for a romantic walk by the creek.'

'We'll be in the smoke-house,' Sam said. 'Eight o'clock. Don't leave me there too long with him.'

Now she just had to figure out a way to make it happen.

There was a faint line of light above the eastern horizon when she eventually made it home. The frosted ground was starting to shine as if a million tiny diamonds were embedded in the earth. She settled the horse in the stable and crossed quietly to the house.

The kitchen door creaked as she opened it, but the room was deserted. She crept along the hallway holding her breath. For a moment she thought she heard footsteps. She froze. There was nothing. She opened the door to her own room, stepped inside, closed the door, and only then let the air slip from her lungs. The dawn was lighting up the sky beyond her thin curtains. She lay on her bed and closed her eyes. She couldn't ever remember being this tired. Within moments she was asleep, a dreamless sleep, a sleep not hounded by worries or concerns, an exhausted sleep.

She never heard Henry Young open her door and step quietly inside. Never noticed him standing at the end of her bed looking down at her. Never saw the mean look on his bruised face.

She was unaware of all of this until he reached out and cruelly twisted one of her still-booted feet, bringing her back to consciousness with a cry on her lips.

She was instantly fearful. His face was more bruised than she had imagined it would be. It looked as though her kick had split his lip, too.

'What are you doing in here?' she said, deciding that attack was the best form of defence.

He said nothing. He just stared at her, breathing slowly and loudly. She noticed he was clenching and unclenching his fists, stretching his fingers in-between the clenches. She stared back, trying to match his hard look.

'Did you find him?' he said at last.

She looked at him, her mind racing, trying to formulate a story. She nodded.

'And?'

'You know what they'd set out to do. Why ask?'

His lips curled into a slight smile. He raised his thumb and pressed it against the scab on his lower lip.

'They hung him,' she said.

His smile widened and he nodded.

'Don't,' she said, still on the offensive. 'Don't smile. Don't laugh. In fact don't even speak. Just go.'

But he ignored her. 'It was no more than he deserved.'

'No one deserves that. They dragged him from his bed and took him away.'

'He was a killer.'

'You *knew* they were going to do it.'

He rubbed his chin and continued to smile. Eventually he left. Knowing that they had hanged the Angelo boy seemed to be enough. A split lip and a bruised face was a small price to pay, Sam guessed. After he'd gone she breathed a sigh of relief and closed her eyes again. Sometime later Henry might get to hear about how Casey hadn't been hanged, or at least, how his body was gone. But that didn't matter. If he mentioned this she'd plead ignorance and tell him how she saw the boys stringing Casey up and then running away.

102

Despite these thoughts and her still-racing heart she was so tired that sleep came easily once more.

It wasn't until late afternoon that she managed to track Milton down and catch him alone. He had been with Hudson, Campbell, and John Stark for much of the day. She guessed they must have stayed up late too – past dawn, no doubt – and eventually dossed down in the bunkhouse mid-morning. She saw him stumbling up from the trees on the east side of the ranch, buttoning his pants. The wind had dropped and though the ground was still white in places the temperature felt warm in comparison with the previous few days.

'Milton,' she said, smiling. 'Can I have a word?'

He looked bad. His eyes were bloodshot and his skin drawn and dirty. She could smell the sweat on him. It was hard to maintain the smile.

'Sam,' he said. There was no life in his voice. He looked worn out. And, she thought, a little scared – like maybe he'd seen a ghost. That helped her with the smile. Later, she thought, we'll rustle up another spirit to scare you even more.

'I've been wanting to talk to you for a while.'

He looked at her suspiciously.

'Why would you want to talk to me?'

'Just . . . just because,' she said.

'Huh?'

'You're on your own?' she said.

'The boys are in the bunkhouse.'

'No. I mean, you don't have anyone?'

'No.'

'Don't you ever wish you could just talk to someone. Someone who could understand?'

He still had suspicion in his eyes. 'You've got your ma. And Henry.'

'And you've got the boys. But it's not the same, is it?'

He thought about that for a moment, picking at his teeth with a dark thumbnail.

'I heard you rode out of town with Casey Angelo yesterday,' he said then.

'Who told you that?'

'Nez Sully mentioned it.'

She nodded. 'A strange boy. Casey, that is, not Sully. He wanted to see the place where his father was shot. It was on my way so I offered to show him.'

'You talk to him?'

She shook her head. 'He was quiet and moody. Kept talking about his father.'

'An eye for an eye,' Milton said.

'What's that?'

'That's what he told me yesterday. He was after revenge for his daddy.'

'An eye for an eye,' she said quietly. 'There's talk that he killed someone. A girl from town.'

'He did.'

'Maybe that's why he was so quiet.'

'Did you like him?'

'No. He was too moody and quiet.'

'You seen him today?'

'No. I've not been out. Why?'

'No reason.'

'Listen Milton, are you going to be around later?' She folded her arms as she asked this question, pressing her breasts together, and smiled again. 'I've got a ton of chores to do right now but I'd like to talk some more.'

He pursed his lips, moving them one way and then the other. It made his nose twitch and he looked more rodent-like than ever. She saw his eyes flicker down to her chest, linger, and then return to her face.

'I was going to go to town,' he said. 'There's some business to sort out.'

She felt a pang of alarm. 'It won't take long. I just . . . it's been so long since I've talked to anyone out of the family.' She squeezed her folded arms together even further.

'Well, maybe for a little while.'

'How about quarter to eight in the smoke-house. It'll be warm . . . and private.'

He ran a pink tongue over his lips and nodded slowly.

'Back in the coffin,' Hap said.

'Isn't there anywhere else?' Casey said. The coffin was a little too tight and too warm. It made his mind run a little too fast, as well.

'No. There's no time. In you get.'

Once he was safely entombed he tried to slow his breathing and quieten his heart. He could hear Hap and Hudson.

'Anyone brought you a body in this morning?' Hudson said. His footsteps were heavy and close as he barged his way into Hap's back room.

'There's been no new business since poor Suzie Cobb met her unfortunate demise.'

'Are you sure?' Hudson was still walking around. He sounded awfully close.

'It's one of the things about my job,' Hap said. 'You tend to remember if you've got any new customers.'

'Don't get smart with me. I'm not in the mood.'

Then Casey heard the sound of a coffin lid being slid open. His heart picked up speed again and he tensed himself, wondering how quickly he'd be able to spring upwards from his supine position and how quickly his eyes would adjust to the light. He cursed himself for not having a gun. But his .45 was back under his bed at Martha Slade's. At least he hoped that was where it was. If all went according to plan he'd be needing it pretty soon.

'There's no one in here,' Hap said, remarkably calmly, Casey thought. 'Is it anyone in particular you're looking for?'

'I just heard a rumour that someone . . .'

'That someone what?'

'Nothing. But you let me know if anyone turns up.' Hudson's footsteps moved away and Casey let out a silent sigh of relief.

'I'll do that,' Hap said. 'Will we be seeing you at Suzie's funeral?'

'I doubt it,' Hudson said.

Even sealed in the casket Casey felt the cold wind as Hudson opened the door and stepped outside.

'I'll get your father's clothes,' Hap said.

'I'll come with you.'

'No.'

'I insist.'

'No,' Hap said. 'I'll do it.'

'I'd like to see him.'

'Remember him as he was, Casey.'

'I'll always remember him as he was, Hap. But this is something I need to do.'

'No, it's not. It's something you feel you *ought* to do.'

'Hap.'

'No arguments. You're meant to be in hiding, anyway.'

Casey sighed. Hap was right. He didn't really want to be the one to strip the blood-soaked shirt off his father's back but it did seem to be one of those tasks that ought to be undertaken by a son.

'I'm the undertaker,' Hap went on. 'I've already had his shirt off once.'

'You have?'

Hap nodded.

'Sit here. Roll a cigarette. I won't be long.'

'I don't mind doing it,' Casey said.

'I know you don't. You're a brave one, Casey.'

'I'm only doing what anyone would do.'

'I don't think many people would have done what you've done.'

'I've not done anything yet.'

Hap smiled. 'You just came into town, caused a little havoc, swept the prettiest girl off her feet and got yourself lynched. Now you're going to dress up as a ghost and put yourself in the firing-line once again. It isn't much, is it?'

Despite the occasion Casey smiled too.

'Put like that I guess I have been a bit busy.'

'Have you thought about what's going to happen tonight?'

'How do you mean?'

'What happens if Milton's reaction is to put a few more bullets into your father. Or rather, you.'

'He won't do that.'

'Are you sure?'

'No. But that's my bet and I'm sticking with it.'

Hap nodded.

'Roll that cigarette, Casey. I'll be right back.'

The clothes were ice cold. Hap hung them on the back of chairs around the stove, the dark coat and the yellow shirt with two bullet holes in it. The holes were kind of confusing. They made Casey sad and then they made him mad, they made him sorrowful and determined. And in one strange way he was glad they were there because it was the dark bloodstained patches contrasting with the unusual yellow shirt that was going to convince Milton that he was indeed seeing Robert Angelo. That was, Casey thought with a touch of anxiety, if Milton had been there in the first place. That was part of Casey's gamble. Everything he had learned and felt so far indicated that Milton had played a crucial part in the murder. Oh, they were all guilty. Casey had no doubt about that. But it was Milton who seemed most on edge, as if it was he who had most to lose. Though Casey still recalled the marshal telling him that of them all it was John Stark who was the marksman.

As dusk closed in outside Hap flicked open his pocket-watch.

'I guess it's time to get dressed,' he said.

Casey nodded and stood up. He felt more nervous than he had at any time since he'd come back to Tyburn Ridge. When he thought he was going to die the night before he hadn't been nervous. He'd been scared then, terrified, even. But there'd been no time for nerves. Now it was different. Now he was stepping into his father's shoes both literally and figuratively and he was nervous he wasn't going to be up to the job.

Hap seemed to read his mind.

'They're going to fit you like a glove,' he said. 'In all ways.'

'Let's do it,' Casey said.

CHAPTER TEN

Milton had dressed up for the occasion. That didn't actually mean much. He didn't have a nice suit tucked away, just a shirt that was a little less dirty and creased than the one he'd been wearing for the past week. But the fact that he'd made an effort wasn't lost on Sam. Milton must have had an idea about what her suggested intentions were all about – indeed, she'd led him along that path with some subtle (and not so subtle) body language and now she was hoping that she wasn't going to live to regret it. He was five minutes early, too. It was twenty minutes until eight o'clock. Twenty minutes to keep him talking and at arm's length and to pray that Casey and Hap turned up on time. Or even turned up at all. There was a score of reasons that they mightn't make it – not least was that Marshal Horn might have managed to locate and even arrest Casey.

Thinking of Casey made Sam realize something else: Milton was wearing his gun. She didn't know whether Casey would be wearing one. She assumed so, though he hadn't had one when they'd ridden through the snowstorm together the day before. And even if he was packing a gun, was he any good with it? There was an air of confidence about him but she was sure Hap had been kept very busy over the years with men who'd had an air of confidence but a slow hand. So she decided she'd have to stick close by Milton, maybe make out she was scared too, and

109

if he went for his gun she would have to knock it out of his hand or at least spoil his aim.

Luckily the smoke-house was warm but not overly smoky. It wouldn't have been the ideal place to have met a man had she had any true romantic interest. But on a freezing evening when she knew she wouldn't be there long it would suffice.

'So,' Milton said, pulling the door closed behind him, and smiling.

She smiled back. 'Just leave it open a little ways, Milton. It's not smoky but it still smells a little in here.'

'It's a nice smell,' he said. 'Won't someone wonder what's going on if they see the door is open. They might even see in.'

'There's nothing going on.'

A puzzled look crossed his face. 'I thought . . .'

'Don't you just want someone to talk to sometimes, Milton?'

'We've been through this, this afternoon. You ain't been keen on talking to me for many months. Not ever, in fact.'

'Come on, sit down.' She'd laid a thick blanket on the floor. 'I've even brought some whiskey.'

Now his eyes lit up. 'That's more like it.'

She sat down and tucked her skirt around her legs.

'You don't have to do that,' he said, reaching over to touch the edge of her skirt where it covered her leg.

'Drink?' she said.

He moved his hand away reluctantly. She wondered how many minutes had passed.

Milton took a long swig, wiped his mouth with the back of his hand, and then offered the bottle to Sam.

'No, it's OK, thanks.'

'Go on. It'll warm you up.'

'I brought it for you.'

'And I'm offering it to you.'

She smiled and took the bottle, wiping the top carefully before taking a small drink. He was right. It did warm her. Made her shiver, too.

'That's good.'

He moved a little closer, the shadows on his face dancing in the light of the lantern that she'd brought into the smoke-house.

'So why d'you change your mind?' he asked, letting his hand rest on her leg. This time she didn't say anything. She wondered what time it was and what would happen if Casey was late, or, God forbid, if for some reason he couldn't get here.

'What time do you have to go to town?'

'Maybe I don't have to go at all.' He moved his hand slightly.

'There's no rush,' she said.

'No rush to do what?'

'To do anything.'

'You didn't answer my question,' he said.

'What question was that?'

'Why d'you change your mind?'

'I didn't.'

'You didn't, huh?' Now he caught a piece of her dress in between his thumb and finger and pulled it from beneath her leg. 'I thought you didn't like me.'

'I've never felt ... I've never thought about it too much, Milton. It's just recently ... I've just been wanting someone to talk to.'

'Talk, huh?' Now he was pulling her dress up over her ankle, revealing bare skin.

'Mmm,' she said.

'And what Hudson said wasn't true?'

'What did he say?' Milton was rubbing her ankle with his thumb now. In the flickering light she saw him lick his

111

lips, his thin pink tongue flicking in and out. She wondered if there were rats in the smoke-house.

'He said you didn't like me.'

She shook her head. 'I wasn't interested in anyone.'

'But now . . .'

'I can't explain it.'

He smiled. 'I understand. We all got needs.'

Sam tried to see through the crack in the door. What time was it? Where was Casey? What would happen if he didn't arrive?

'More whiskey?' Milton asked her, a sly grin on his wet lips.

'Thank you.' She took a small sip and handed the bottle to him. He drank long and fast again. When he lowered the bottle she was amazed to see that it was a third empty. He'd only taken two swigs. Maybe, she thought, he's building up courage. *Come on, Casey*, she urged silently.

'Makes you feel good, don't it?' he said.

Suddenly, amongst the rising revulsion and panic, a moment of inspiration appeared.

'You heard about what happened at Hap's?'

'No.'

'They say someone – some*thing*, I guess – broke open one of his coffins.'

Milton didn't look overly impressed. He was more interested in her ankle and hitching her skirt up another inch. It took all her will power not to snatch her leg away.

'Who said?' he asked, his fingers slipping under the material and touching her calf. 'Smooth,' he whispered, almost as if he was in a world of his own.

'It's the rumour in town.'

'You been to town, today?' He moved one of his legs, making himself more comfortable. She wished she could have done the same.

'No. Henry told me.'

'Henry ain't been in town, neither.'

'Lordy,' she said. 'Ain't you a one? I don't know who told Henry. All I know is he told me and said that it's the talk of the town.'

'That someone broke open a coffin at Hap's?'

'Yep.'

'It don't sound like no big deal to me. Was it outside?' She nodded.

'Then it was probably a dog.'

'You don't understand, Milton.'

'What don't I understand?'

'They said that it looked like it had been broken open *from the inside.*' That got him. The small circles he was tracing on her leg stopped and he looked up at her face.

'What?'

'Something broke open a coffin,' she said. 'And the talk is it then climbed out.'

In the lamplight it was hard to tell if Milton had turned any more pale than usual but certainly the way he had tensed up told her that she had at last reached through to him.

'That ain't possible,' he said.

'I'm only saying what I heard.'

'No.'

'It's a full moon, too,' she said. She'd noticed earlier as she'd made her way towards the smoke-house.

'Full moon?'

'The Indians used to believe that the full moon sucked the spirits up out of the ground,' she said. She had no idea of whether this was true or not but her words had hit home. Milton was stretching and clenching his fingers, then clasping them together and then letting them go like a man who couldn't decide whether he was a piano-player or a priest.

'You know, I think I might have to go into town after

all.' His voice sounded a mite unsteady now.

'*Now?*'

'Yep.' He took another long swig of whiskey. She felt panic rising inside her. She was meant to keep him here until eight o'clock.

'Aren't you enjoying this?'

He tried to smile. 'I could come and see you later. I know where your room is.'

'No, you can't come in there.'

'Back out here, then?' He was clambering to his feet. 'I gotta go.'

'What time will you be back?'

'I don't know. We definitely got some unfinished business, don't we?' But then he was hitching up his trousers and stepping out into the night.

Casey sat atop one of Hap's horses and looked across the Ranier yard at the smoke-house. There was a faint light flickering through the slightly open door and it made him feel angry when he thought about what might be happening inside. Sam had told them that Milton was always asking her to go walking with him and Casey couldn't bear to think of his ratlike lips touching Sam. Not that she'd let him kiss her, of course. He was sure of that. But no matter how much he tried to convince himself of this the thought still kept jumping to the forefront of his mind. It even submerged the fear that was bubbling through his blood. He knew Milton was in the smoke-house. All he had to do now was to ride across the yard and make his presence – or rather, his father's presence – known to Milton. But what he didn't know was where Hudson was. Or Campbell James or John Stark. He and Hap had skirted the Ranier property and had come upon the smoke-house from the back. There was shelter here from a small copse of trees. The plan was to come out of the trees, call Milton out of the shed and scare him half-way to hell. Then they'd ask him why he'd murdered Robert Angelo. His reaction would tell them all they needed to know. The plan had seemed fine until right now. What would happen if Hudson or Campbell came out of the bunkhouse just at the wrong moment? What would happen if Milton said nothing? What would happen if he simply wasn't scared?

Hap had told him that he was the spit of his father, especially dressed up in his shirt and suit. The bullet holes were the ultimate convincer.

'If he don't believe he's seeing a ghost then the man's a fool,' Hap had said.

'The man is a fool,' Casey had said.

'You move like him, Casey. You ride like him. You talk like him. Don't worry. If Milton had anything to do with your father's death we'll know it.'

The full moon added to the atmosphere. It was still rising behind the trees in which Casey sat motionless. There was even a low ground mist, settling and freezing.

It was time.

Milton came out into the cold air. He couldn't believe how a night could turn bad so quickly. One moment he had been running his hand all the way up Samantha Ranier's leg. *All the way*. Wait until he told Campbell! Boy, he'd been hot in there. It had been her idea, too, even if she did seem a bit nervous and unsure of what to do. But all those times with Suzie and Polly-Anne at Sloppy's had given him the experience he'd need to bring Sam to just where he wanted her. And there'd be plenty of time for it, too, now that she'd seen the light and had realized what a catch he was. Not that he actually wanted to be caught, but she didn't have to know that. Not for a good length of time anyway.

But then why did she suddenly have to go and tell him

that other stuff? One moment he was simply savouring the velvet touch of her skin and the next she went and swept it all away all by mentioning what had happened at Hap's. He'd gone from hot to cold and back again in about two seconds and was instantly a long way from thinking about Samantha's leg. Something weird was going on. Samantha didn't know it, which was why he was going to have to sweet talk her all over again, but something bad was about. First of all they put two bullets into Robert Angelo.

'Justice,' Hudson had told them afterwards. 'Ten years, but I never forgot. I knew this day was going to come.'

And then little Yellow Casey comes back to town. Only he wasn't so little any more and, to be honest, he didn't seem so yellow either. And he can't help but keep sniffing around either. It seemed like a good idea to lynch him. Hudson was all for it. John Stark said it was poetic, too. Like the closing of a circle, on account of they'd done the same thing to Casey all those years ago.

'My mama had to live through hell,' Hudson said. 'Let's see how *his* mama likes it.' They should have stayed and watched Casey hang but it was part of the plan to just leave him there. It must have been an awful way to die, helpless and alone. 'Cept he hadn't died helpless and alone. Or had he? No one knew. He'd just disappeared like a ghost. There was no way he could have escaped. He *must* be dead. But now . . . now something had broken out of a coffin at Hap's. Broken out from the inside. It had to be Robert Angelo. No one else was dead. Well, save for Suzie. He supposed it could have been her. Hell, maybe it was both of them. It was a full moon and, like Sam said, the full moon sucked the spirits back up out of their graves. He had to get to town and find Hudson and Campbell quick. Tell 'em what he knew. Find out what they'd heard. Maybe go see Hap, see what the story really was.

He finished tightening his belt, shivered and looked up.

'No,' he said. His mouth dropped open. 'Jesus.'

Robert Angelo sat before him on a black horse. There was mist rising around the horse's fetlocks and huge clouds of freezing vapour came from its nose as it breathed. The moon, full and low, shone through the horse's breath making it glow a dark orange. On top of the horse Robert Angelo sat still and motionless. He looked taller than he had when Milton and John Stark had waited on the trail for him. But back then they had been looking down on him, now he had the high ground. Angelo wasn't quite silhouetted, he was turned slightly into the moonlight and Milton could clearly see the holes in his yellow shirt that still dripped blood. It wasn't possible. Yet the man they had killed was right there in front of him.

'Milton Craig,' Angelo said, his voice soft yet hoarse as if no water had passed his throat in days. Angelo turned slowly to face Milton. Angelo's hat was pulled down low. Milton couldn't see the ghost's eyes but he had no doubt that had he been able to they would have been black pits or fiery red orbs.

'No,' Milton said, again. He wanted to reach down for his revolver but his hands refused to obey his brain's orders.

'You're the one,' Angelo said, and started to pull a rifle from his saddle sheath.

'No!' Milton said. 'It wasn't me.' He heard the door of the smoke house squeaking open behind him. He knew he ought to turn and tell Samantha to stay inside but he was more concerned with saving his own skin than hers.

Angelo nodded. 'You were there.'

The rifle was clear of the saddle now and Angelo was swinging it upwards.

'I never fired the bullets!'

117

The rifle started to level on Milton. He felt his belly tingling and had to squeeze his buttocks together. Even so he still felt a drop of urine dribble loose.

'It was John Stark!'

Angelo worked the rifle action.

'It wasn't me! It was Hudson's idea.'

'You were there.'

Now the dribble of urine became a flow.

'I . . . I . . . Please!'

Milton stared into the dark barrel of the silhouetted rifle. He was vaguely aware that he had wet himself and that Samantha was behind him, but that didn't seem to matter. He knew he was about to die. Again he tried desperately to move his hand towards his gun but though his hand shook and shuddered it wouldn't move towards his holster.

'Don't bother, Milton,' Angelo said, his voice just a whisper now. 'I'm already dead.'

'*Please*! It was John Stark!'

'Close your eyes, Milton.' Angelo's horse fidgeted, it snorted and now it looked like orange smoke being expelled from its lungs. The dark rider had his finger on the rifle's trigger.

'Please . . .'

'Your eyes.'

Milton closed his eyes.

'On your knees.'

Milton fell to his knees, sobbing.

He waited and waited.

But when he looked up Robert Angelo was gone.

Casey said, 'Is that enough proof for you, Hap?'

'It's enough for *me*.'

'But?'

Casey looked across at the man riding alongside him.

118

The full moon was still rising but there were clouds scudding across in front of it and for a moment the undertaker's face was too dark to read.

'But nothing.'

'You don't think it's enough for Horn, do you?'

Hap shook his head. 'I'm not sure. The stakes are high, Casey.'

'The stakes have always been high, Hap. I told you, I didn't just come here to collect my father. From day one I vowed I would make someone pay for killing him. I have my proof now.'

Now Hap nodded. 'I know. But when you've seen as many dead men as I have, Casey, it makes you stop and think sometimes.'

'I have witnesses. You're my witness. Sam's my witness. Lordy, Hap. People are hung everyday out on the frontier with *no* witnesses.'

'I just want you to be careful.'

'I've been careful every step of the way.'

'You've done well. I don't want to see you blow it now.'

Casey smiled in the darkness.

'Don't worry. Milton will be as shocked to see me as he was to see my daddy. Only it's going to be in Sloppy's in the middle of the day. There'll be plenty of people around to hear him admit to what he told my father.'

'How do you know that he'll be there?'

'They'll all be there.'

'You're sure?'

'I'm going to ask them. Simple as that. You think if they get word that Casey Angelo wants to see them they're not going to turn up?'

Hap laughed. But he cut the laugh short.

'And then what?'

'I do what I came to do.'

*

There was something in his pocket and there was something on his mind. Both were inextricably linked and both hovered on the periphery of his thoughts as he rode, nagging him like a tooth with a small, painless, but annoying hole in it. He had heard and felt the piece of paper crinkle as he had slipped his father's jacket on earlier. Hap must have missed it when he'd checked Robert Angelo's pockets. Maybe he'd simply patted down the clothes rather than going through the pockets in detail. Casey had intended taking a look at the paper right away but Hap had been there straightening the coat, pulling the buttons together, adjusting the hat, and telling him to stand and to move just so. Then he'd asked Casey to talk to him and though Casey's voice, already gravelly from the hanging, needed little disguising to make him sound just like his father Hap made him practise whispering for several minutes. They'd gone through what Casey would say and do. They'd discussed back-up plans in case everything went wrong, in case Milton had come out of the smokehouse shooting, in case any of the other cowboys turned up. And by the time they'd saddled up Hap's two horses the paper that Casey's fingers had found had slipped down his list of priorities. He hadn't thought about it again until it was all over, until they had left Milton weeping on the ground, and had faded away into the night. On the long circular ride back to town – not the normal route because they hadn't wanted to be seen – Casey had remembered the paper. It was too cold for him to undo his coat out there on the trail. His hands were encased in thick gloves. And it would have been too dark to read anything anyway. But now he was itching to get back to Hap's and to go through his father's pockets.

Because the other thing that was on his mind was the question of what had made Robert Angelo return to Tyburn Ridge in the first place?

*

Sam arrived in Tyburn Ridge about thirty minutes after Casey and Hap, who were sat at the table already nursing whiskey-laden coffee when she arrived. They were staring at a piece of crumpled paper.

'What is it?' she asked. She'd expected them to be in a good mood following Milton's confession.

Hap stood up to pour her a coffee. Casey pushed the paper across the table towards her.

'It's from your mother,' he said, his voice weary and downbeat.

'What?' She picked up the paper and read it aloud.

' "Robert, please come quick. I'm in trouble and I need help. You're all I can think of. If the past means anything to you then come quick. Violet." And three kisses.' The words were written carefully in black ink. The paper was thick and of good quality.

Hap handed Sam a mug of coffee. She hadn't even taken her coat off. 'Where's this from?'

'It was in his pocket,' Hap said. Casey was staring into the steam rising off his own drink. His hat was on the table next to his cup. His dark hair was tousled.

'Robert's pocket?'

Casey looked up at her. 'It was why he came back.'

Sam sat down. She looked at the paper again. There was something wrong with it.

'What does it mean?' Casey asked before Sam could figure out what was bothering her. ' "If the past means anything to you then come quick." And what are those kisses about?'

Sam covered her face with her hands, pressing her fingertips into her eyes. Then she sighed and lowered her hands. 'Don't you know?' she asked.

'Know what?'

121

'Your father was going to marry my mother,' she said.

His eyes flashed angrily at her.

'No! My father . . . my mother. They're very happy.' He paused and then corrected himself. 'They *were* very happy.'

'I know that, Casey.'

'They were still in love.'

'I know.'

'Then . . .'

'She doesn't mean he was coming *back* here to marry her, Casey,' Hap said. 'Look at the note again.'

'I've done nothing but look at it for twenty minutes.'

' "If the past means anything to you then come quick." ' Hap said.

Casey ran a hand through his hair. Sam saw now why it was so tousled. He looked at her.

'He was going to marry her a long time ago?'

She nodded. She felt a few tears spring into her eyes. It was a sad moment and she wasn't quite sure why?

Casey sat quietly for a few moments then looked up.

'Are you all right?'

'I'm fine. I guess we don't always consider our parents and their pasts and their broken hearts.'

He nodded, still trying to get everything straight in his mind.

'I can't imagine – I guess I don't want to imagine – anyone with my father but my mother.'

'I know what you mean.'

'What happened? When was this? Who broke it off?'

Sam shook her head. 'I don't know. It was a long time ago.'

'You never mentioned it two days ago when we were catching up.'

'It's awkward. Like you said: you don't want to imagine anyone with your father but your mother.'

'He must have loved her a great deal to come back,' Hap said.

'I don't know,' Sam said. 'I know very little about it. I only learned this much a few days ago.'

'What do you mean?'

'My mother's been having these deep conversations with me recently. Trying to get me interested in finding a man. She told me only a week or two ago that she almost got married to someone else before my father.'

'*My* father?'

'Yes. It took a lot of persuading for her to tell me who it was. But I think she wanted me to know. I think she was quite proud of the fact that he loved her.'

'He was a fine man,' Hap said. 'Why didn't the marriage happen?'

'I don't know. She wouldn't say. I guess either way – whether she broke it off or whether she was jilted – it ruins the fairy tale.'

'So what is this trouble of which she wrote?' Hap asked.

Now the thing that was bothering her about the note became horribly clear.

'There is no trouble,' Sam said. 'This isn't my mother's writing.'

CHAPTER ELEVEN

Early the next morning Casey Angelo knocked on Martha Slade's door. The street was deserted. The day before it had hardly snowed and the night had been more mild than previous nights. Already there was enough cloud cover to suggest that this day would be warmer than others had been recently. Maybe spring was coming and maybe by noon, when Sloppy's opened, the sun would have burned the clouds away and Casey would feel the warmth on his back as he took the vengeance he had come for.

Martha opened the door in a heavy woollen dressing gown.

'You!' she said.

He put on his best charming smile.

'I'm sorry I've not been around much,' he said. 'I guess I'm a poor customer.'

She stared at him. He couldn't tell whether she was angry or pleased to see him.

'May I come in?' he said. 'I believe I still have a room here.'

She stood aside and then closed the door behind him.

'I had the marshal here yesterday looking for you,' she said. 'And then Hudson Ranier.'

'I'm sorry for the bother.'

'It's no bother, but I think I'm owed an explanation.'

'Are my things still here?'

'Yes. But—'

'I'll just go upstairs then. There's something I need.'

'What's going on? Are you in trouble? Is it to do with Suzie Cobb? I'll call the marshal!'

Casey didn't want to spend his last few hours in town dodging the marshal.

'Martha, I'm not in trouble but it is true that the marshal wants me out of town. That's why he came to see you yesterday. I bet he was waiting on the train platform to wave goodbye to me. When I didn't turn up he came looking for me. But there's no need to call him. He'll be getting his wish. I'll be leaving in the morning. One more day, that's all.'

'It certainly sounds like trouble.'

'I've told you the truth all along, Martha. Somebody killed my father and I came here to bring him home.' He sighed and decided he might as well tell her all of it. 'But I didn't *just* come here to bring him home. I wanted to find out who killed him. And why.'

'And you've found out?'

'Yes I have.'

She put a hand over her mouth.

'I'll just get a few things,' he said. 'I promise I won't be a bother to you any more, I promise.'

'What are you going to do?' she asked.

'I'm going to do what any good son would do.'

'Are you going to kill them?'

'That depends on them,' he said.

There was something odd about Casey. Hap had noticed it the night they had tried to hang him, or rather the next day. Now he realized what it was – he was acting and looking more and more like his father. He spoke like him, used the same words, moved the same slow and easy way. Hap remembered the day that Robert Angelo had brought

125

Spencer Ranier in. It had been a tense day all round. There could have been a lot of shooting, a lot of killing. But Robert Angelo had given off an aura of power, of invincibility, and had gone about his work slowly and surely. And without bloodshed. Casey was giving off that same aura now. Like father, like son, Hap thought, and felt good with the knowledge. Though he suspected it didn't bode well for Hudson and his gang.

'I'd like you to do a favour for me,' Casey told Hap that morning.

'Of course.'

'You too, Sam.'

They were back in Hap's kitchen drinking coffee. It had been another long night. Casey had spent most of it awake, his father's Colt on his lap. Who knew where Milton had gone or what he was planning to do after they had scared him half to death. If he had rounded up Hudson and Campbell and John Stark it would be pretty likely that the four of them would have marched on Hap's, determined to find out what was happening to people who were meant to be dead. So despite the day ahead Casey had stayed awake guarding Hap and Sam – both innocent parties whom he had dragged into his mission of vengeance at Tyburn Ridge. Now Casey was eating fried bacon and dismantling and cleaning the gun he had just collected from Martha's. He'd decided that he ought to use his own gun this coming day. There would have been a poetic justice in using his father's gun but the time had come to be professional not poetic, and it was with his own .45 that he was most at home.

'Sure,' Sam said. 'Ask away.' Neither she nor Hap were eating.

'I'd like you to put out word that Casey Angelo would like to meet Hudson Ranier and his boys. I guess you know who to tell this to so that it'll get through to them.' He was reassembling the gun as he spoke, not even looking at his fingers as he worked.

'Sully's will be a good place to start. Anything you tell to Nez Sully has got a way of spreading like wildfire.'

'I know that.'

'And there are a couple of other gossips in town, too,' Sam said.

'Tell them Casey Angelo said noon in Sloppy's.'

Hap flicked open his pocket-watch and nodded. Part of him was nervous, but seeing Casey this way, the confidence and swagger and aura about him, he figured he'd more likely be measuring Hudson or Milton up for a coffin than Casey.

'Marshal Horn's liable to hear about it, too.'

'Good. If he's in Sloppy's too then he'll hear what I have to say.'

'He might try and stop you.'

'Nobody's going to stop me now.'

'I believe you,' Hap said.

Sam stood up. 'You're sure about this, aren't you, Casey? I mean, you can still just walk away.'

'There was never a moment when I could just walk away.'

She nodded. Hap was watching her closely too. He couldn't quite fathom the look in her eyes. Was it loneliness? Fear? He didn't think it was either. It was almost a regret, as though she'd resigned herself to something bad happening and didn't like herself for it. He wondered whether it was her brother she was worried for rather than Casey? Or was it for both of them. Because, for Sam, there could be no winners this morning.

'Then I guess we'd better get the gossips fired up and talking,' she said, and forced a smile. 'High noon in Sloppy's.'

Casey nodded. 'Be careful, Sam.'

'I will be.'

She stepped outside and closed the door. For a moment a cold whisper of air made both Hap and Casey shiver. They looked at one another for a long time. The time for talking was over. Now it was a question of waiting. And then finishing the job that had been started. But the silence was too hard for Hap.

'Are you going to kill her brother, Casey?' he asked at last.

Another moment stretched between them but before Casey could answer there was the sound of shouting in the street and the echo of a gunshot.

Milton was waiting for her outside. She didn't know whether he'd been prowling up and down Tyburn Ridge trying to find her or if he'd known where she was and had simply holed up outside Hap's. What she did know was that he had the wild red-eyed look of a man who had missed too much sleep over the last few days. He smelled bad, too. Alcohol and sweat and tobacco. She was no more than ten yards down the plank-walk when he swung out from the shadows and caught her arm.

'You tricked me, bitch!' he said, and his fingers dug deep into her arm even through her heavy coat.

She tried to twist away from him but his grip was too tight.

'You never liked me,' he said. And then followed this with: 'That wasn't Robert Angelo last night. That was Casey dressed up.' Even as she struggled to free herself, somewhere deep inside the order of his words struck her as strange. It was as if the fact that she had pretended to like him was more of an affront than the fact they had tricked him into revealing that John Stark had been the killer.

He was dragging her across the street now. She tried to

hit him with her free hand but the angle was wrong and there was no strength in her blow. The second time, instead of trying to hit him, she raked his face with her fingernails. She felt his skin tear but he didn't even flinch.

Now she tried to call out for Casey and Hap. But her voice was weak with fear and it just seemed to roll along the quiet and empty street, making no more noise than tumbleweed.

'Shut your mouth,' he said.

She tried to call louder. It was better but it still wasn't loud enough.

And now he hit her. He let go of her arm for an instant and before she even realized that she was free he had swung around and caught her square on the mouth. Nobody had ever hit her that hard before. Everything blurred for a moment. She felt dizzy and unsteady and then her legs gave way and she sank to the floor.

'I told you not to shout,' he said, bending over her. For a moment there appeared to be two Miltons looking down at her. Then three. All of them had stars dancing around their heads. Now they coalesced into a single entity and she saw that he had a knife in his hand. The blade flashed in the low cold sunlight and she had a vision of him running the blade across her cheeks like she'd heard he did to a boy named Tom Murphy many years before.

'No,' she said.

'I thought you liked me.'

'I do.'

'No. You tricked me. You all tricked me.'

She wanted to cry out again. She was surely still close enough to Hap's for them to hear, but now the blade was silencing her.

'You're drunk,' she said.

'Maybe. So what?'

'You don't know what you're saying.'

129

'I'm going to cut your face,' he said. 'I've been waiting all night to cut your face.'

There was no arguing with him. He leant closer. She pushed her feet into the hard packed dirt of the road and tried to scramble clear of him but he simple edged forward with her.

'The knife hurts,' he said. 'They all cry and scream but I think it's the scars that hurt more. The knife is just for a few seconds. The scars are for ever.'

Now she did cry out loudly, starting to scream for Casey and Hap, but her words were cut short as Milton dropped a knee down on to her stomach and all the wind was knocked out of her. The last thing she saw before she closed her eyes was that he was crying.

It had all gone wrong for Hudson Ranier. This should have been so simple. He had been waiting ten years for an opportunity to entice Robert Angelo into coming back to Tyburn Ridge. Ten long years. Sometimes it felt like he'd never return. Then out of the blue he'd found out that his mother had once been on the verge of marrying the bastard. Once the shock had passed and his mind had started working again he came up with the perfect plan. And indeed it had all been working like a charm. The ex-lawman had come back to the Ridge quicker than a trail hand would find his way upstairs to Suzie Cobb or Polly-Anne. And they had been waiting for him. One watching the train, ready to follow Angelo. Another to ride off and let the two who were setting the ambush know when he was coming. It wasn't too much of an effort. They'd only had to watch two trains. Hudson sent the letter on the east-bound Union Pacific on Wednesday. He'd long known Angelo's address. Going back maybe four years when it had felt as though like he'd never get the chance to trick Angelo into returning he'd made the journey out to

Omaha himself. The itch to kill Angelo had just gotten so bad that he could stand it no longer. So he'd packed his guns and off he went. He hadn't been able to get close enough, though. He wasn't a crack shot and he knew he dare not try it face to face. So he'd come home with even more of a burning desire for vengeance. So the letter went east on Wednesday and on Saturday Robert Angelo came west. Campbell James had cursed Hudson for making him wait on the platform on the Friday.

'It's too soon,' James had said. 'The letter won't even be there yet.' But Hudson had insisted. This was his chance. His only chance. If they had to wait ten days in the cold then so be it, though of course Marshal Horn might have started to get a little interested in them then. When Angelo hadn't arrived on Friday Campbell James was even more indignant. But he'd been at the station again on Saturday and this time Angelo did arrive. He'd brought a horse in the livestock wagon, too. He went into town and took a room, freshened himself up and was then straight off down the trail. Talk about a dog in heat.

Hudson had wanted to pull the trigger himself. That would have been true justice. But unless he could have got within six yards of Angelo, killing him couldn't be guaranteed. So that particular pleasure had fallen to John Stark. It kind of took the edge off things a little but it was still a job well done. Campbell had followed Angelo from the boarding house to the stables and once he saw that Angelo was saddling up he lit out for the ambush site as fast as he could.

It turned out that all four of them had been there at the twist in the trail to see the two bullets hit home and Angelo lying there in the snow, his face twisted in pain. They even stole his horse after he'd died.

It got better.

When they heard on the grapevine that Hap Smith had

sent a telegram to Angelo's boy asking him to come and collect the body they realized that the fun wasn't over yet.

But now it was turning bad. It was Milton's fault. He'd been on edge ever since they'd killed Angelo. First of all he was excited. He'd never been involved in a murder before. He wanted to tell everyone what they'd done. For Hudson, just knowing that he had exacted revenge was enough. For John Stark the feel of the cold trigger beneath his finger and the kick of the gun would have been enough. But Milton had wanted more. The killing had made him feel like a big man and he wanted everyone to know. But after that excitement came fear. Especially when they couldn't find Casey Angelo's body after they'd hung him. Milton was losing it – drinking and not sleeping and starting to imagine Indian spirits raising up out of the ground. Last night he'd told them that he'd seen Angelo's ghost and that the spectre had been going to kill him.

This morning Milton had been drunk and scared and the boys had told him to cool down and sleep it off. Instead he'd said he was going to sort this out once and for all and if they were too scared then that was up to them.

Luckily they'd decided to follow him – maybe make sure he didn't loose off too much. There weren't many folks in town who seemed overly bothered about the fact that a man who had been their sheriff ten years back had been killed, but that didn't mean to say they could have Milton mouthing off about it in public.

Which was how come Hudson was standing across the street with a gun in his hand when Milton took a knife to his sister's face.

'Milton!' Hudson yelled.

Milton looked round. The point of his knife blade was pressed against Sam's cheekbone below her left eye. A drop of blood gathered at the cut and rolled slowly down her face like a red tear.

'You move another muscle and I'll kill you,' Hudson said. He had his revolver drawn but he was too far away. He'd just as likely put a bullet through Samantha as through Milton at this range. Milton would know it too, if he was capable of thinking that far.

'She tricked us,' Milton said. There were tears and blood on his face too. He looked grey and gaunt as if all the worries and fears in his life had risen to the surface in a single night and were eating the life out of him.

'She tricked *you*, Milton. You always were a fool.'

'Don't come any closer!' Milton said.

Hudson stopped. Milton had been drunk when he'd come to see them earlier with his tales of ghosts and spirits and the dead coming back to life. He was still drunk now, by the look of him, but he'd still cottoned on to the fact that Hudson was too far away to shoot him accurately.

'You're a dead man, Milton,' Hudson said.

'I'm your friend,' Milton said. 'We're in this together. We always have been.'

'You let her go right now, then.'

'No.

'It's a simple choice.'

'She tricked us!'

'She tricked you.'

'She made out she loved me.'

'You're a fool, Milton.'

Milton looked down at Samantha. She had her eyes open again and despite her tears she was looking up at him with the same look of longing that she'd used in the smoke-house the previous evening. It was all false. He hated her. She needed to be punished.

'Don't you dare cut her,' Hudson said.

Milton's hand tightened around the knife-blade.

'Milton.'

Now he sobbed.

'Just drop the knife, Milton.'

'No.'

He started to move his hand. Samantha screamed. The sound of a gunshot reverberated across the street and even before the sound had registered Milton lay on his back about six feet from Samantha, a bullet drilled clean through his heart.

Sam didn't open her eyes until she felt her brother's hand clasp her wrist.

'You shouldn't have done it, sis,' she heard Hudson say through the ringing of the gunshot in her ears. She wanted to ask what she shouldn't have done but he was dragging her to her feet and hauling her across the street. Now she saw John Stark standing there on the plank walk with his rifle held in both hands and a tendril of smoke rising from the end of the barrel. She was vaguely aware of doors opening up and down the street, of more voices. She twisted against Hudson's grip and looked back towards Hap's. His was one of the doors that were opening.

Casey burst out on to the street as the last echoes of the gunshot seemed to bounce down off the mountains. He saw everything at once; Milton lying there in the street; The smoke coming from John Stark's gun. Marshal Horn had said that he'd describe John Stark as a marksman. It meant that Milton was probably dead.

'You saved me a bullet,' he whispered and was already raising his gun to fix on Hudson who had hold of Sam's wrist and was pulling her across the street. She looked over her shoulder and for a second their eyes met. There was blood on her face. It was a tough shot but Casey never hesitated. He took aim on the small part of Hudson's back that he could see and started to squeeze the trigger. But the sound of the shot came too soon. A moment later he found himself on his back in the dirt. It felt as though someone had punched him in the shoulder.

Campbell James.

How could I have been so stupid? he thought, even as he rolled instinctively for cover beneath the raised plankwalk. He'd seen Milton lying there, he'd seen John Stark in the shadows, and he'd seen Hudson dragging Sam away. In his haste he'd neglected to cast his eyes around for Campbell.

Another bullet kicked up dirt exactly where he'd been lying two seconds before. There wasn't any pain in his shoulder yet so he quickly rolled even further into the darkness and, still holding his gun in his hand, started to crawl along the ground. Above him he could hear footsteps. Footsteps and screaming. He wondered if the screaming was Sam. Their eyes had met just as Campbell James had shot him. Maybe she thought he was dead. He could hear Hap up there, too, calling his name, sounding confused and worried. And other noises: a dog barking; someone shouting that they ought to get the marshal, that there was a man dead in the street. And then, simultaneous with all this noise, at last came the pain. He'd never been shot before. He didn't know what to expect. At first it had felt like a solid punch. Now it felt as though someone was sticking a knife into his shoulder and twisting it. He gritted his teeth and continued to pull himself forward, only using his good arm – his right arm – to edge towards a gap up ahead in the plank walk. It was an alleyway, he guessed. And trying to reach it now was suddenly slow going. He still held the gun in his hand and had to use his wrist and forearm to pull himself along.

He didn't want to think about what would happen if they'd seen him go down and roll away. But he couldn't help but think about it. They'd likely be waiting for him right where he was headed. He'd stick his head up and they'd blow it clean off.

And that was if he didn't bleed to death first. He pressed his gun hand against his shoulder to see if it would ease the pain and when he took it away it was covered in blood. The gun too.

Nevertheless he pulled himself towards the light ahead. He had no choice. And if he was bleeding to death then so be it. He'd have to worry about it later. As he crawled the voices and footsteps above him became louder and more insistent, once or twice there was someone right above him. Both times he wondered whether it was Campbell James or John Stark and wondered if they were up there looking down at him through the cracks in the wood, tracking his movement with the barrels of their guns, ready to shoot him through the wood and leave him down there for the marshal to drag out later. The second time this happened he rolled over and fixed his gun on the shape above him. If they were going to kill him they were going to get a surprise coming right back.

But out on the street it seemed that confusion reigned. When he finally emerged into the cold light of the alleyway, his Colt at the ready, there was no one there. First he rolled over, then he kneeled, and eventually he pulled himself to his feet and balanced himself against the side of a building. Looking outwards from the alleyway towards Main Street he could just see Milton's boots. Across the street he saw someone run by, holding his hat on his head. Other than that he couldn't see anyone. He figured that he ought to move. Campbell James and John Stark would have seen him go down. They wouldn't know if he was dead or not but they were probably circling already, preparing to make sure. So he set off away from Main Street, down the alleyway to the backs of the buildings. He needed to look at his shoulder, too, but right now getting himself in some place where they wouldn't expect him was even more important.

He ran as best he could in the direction of Hap's. His shoulder sent daggers of pain across his neck and into his chest with every step and when he looked down at the floor he saw that he was leaving a trail of blood. He held his arm up against his chest and that seemed to help. But he knew he was losing too much blood. He had to end this thing soon. The blood-loss would weaken him and he'd need all of his remaining strength and speed now that the killing had started.

He stopped at the next alleyway he came to, took a deep breath, and headed back towards Main Street.

Campbell James saw his bullet hit Casey Angelo in the chest. He saw the boy get knocked to the ground, and he saw him roll under the plank-walk. He didn't know if it had been the force of the bullet that had turned Casey over or if he had simply been rolling for cover. He suspected it was the former. A shot like that, right in the chest, was pretty much guaranteed to kill whoever it hit. He was pleased – ecstatic even – and he looked round to see whether John Stark or Hudson Rainier had seen his marksmanship. Hudson wasn't there. He had been dragging his sister round the back of Sloppy's. She'd caused nothing but trouble these last few days and had pretty much turned Milton's head inside out. In fact, you could say she was more or less responsible for Milton's death. Time would tell how Hudson felt about that. And John Stark hadn't seen the shot either. He'd been looking down, checking something on his gun.

'I got him!' Campbell said.

'Where?'

'I hit him clear in the chest. Knocked him down.'

'Where is he?' They were both crouched down, hiding around the corner of Sloppy's. Now John Stark stood up and peered across the street where Milton's body lay motionless. They saw Hap rushing across to him. Everything seemed to have gone crazy, a dog was barking at the excitement, doors were being opened and closed, and people were screaming and yelling and shouting. 'I don't see him.'

'I hit him so hard he landed all the way under the plank-walk.'

'Did you kill him?'

'Unless he's indestructible, I did.'

'You best go and check.'

'I ain't going over there. You go.'

'What's the matter? If you're so damn sure you killed him you go over and check out that he's dead. It'll only take you a minute. Just wander over and look under the wood.'

'And if he ain't dead?'

'You just said he was.'

'I said I thought he was.'

'Damn, Campbell. Come on, we'll go together.'

The two men stepped out from the shadows and on to the cold hard-packed dirt of Main Street. Already the clouds were thinning and the low sun spread their shadows before them. There were people on the plank-walks on both sides of the road, watching them, whispering about them. The dog had stopped barking and was now sniffing at Milton Craig's body. Hap was kneeling by the body. It seemed like he didn't know which way to look, his head was swivelling in the direction of Sloppy's and then up the street as if he was searching for someone. Now he was looking down at Milton again. As John Stark and Campbell James approached Hap stood up and tried to shoo the dog away but the dog was having none of it and kept on sniffing around Milton's trousers.

'I thought he was your friend,' Hap said. For a man whose living was death, Campbell thought, he sure looked shook up by this particular one.

'He was,' John Stark said.

'But you shot him.'

'He was about to cut Samantha,' Campbell said.

'He'd gone crazy,' John Stark added. 'And what do you do with a crazy dog?'

'Where is Samantha?' There was Hap's head swivelling again.

'Hudson rescued her.'

'Rescued?'

'Yeah, like I said, Milton was about to cut that pretty face of hers.' As they spoke both Campbell and Stark were looking around too, scouring the far side of the street.

'What you looking for?' Hap asked.

'Just looking,' Stark said. 'Don't want any of Milton's friends deciding to exact a little revenge, do we?'

'He didn't have any friends except you boys.'

'One can't be too careful.'

'Someone's gone to get the marshal,' Hap said. 'He should be here any moment.'

'I imagine he'll thank us for saving Samantha's looks.'

'We'll see,' Hap said.

'Tell me,' John Stark said. 'Was it your house the girl came out of? And was Casey Angelo in there too?'

'Where is Casey?' Hap asked.

'He's probably hiding,' Campbell James said, grinning. 'The first sound of gunfire and those yellow ones tend to take cover.'

'You shot him, didn't you? I heard another shot.'

'It was self-defence. He was going for his gun.'

'And he wasn't quick enough,' Stark added.

'Then where is he?' Hap asked. And as he asked the

question he turned his head to look towards the far plank-walk where both Campbell James's and John Stark's eyes were roving. He saw Casey Angelo behind them, maybe thirty yards away. Casey stumbling out on to the Main Street, the left-hand side of his coat dark with blood, his left arm hanging useless beside him. In his right hand, his Colt .45.

'John Stark,' Casey said quietly. Hap didn't know if the quietness was because of his injury or because he wanted to whisper the words. Hap knew that sometimes whispered words carried far more power than those spoken loudly, and indeed it was that way this time. The quiet words floated down Main Street on the almost still air and both Campbell James and John Stark turned simultaneously. 'I heard you killed my father.'

The sun was low, behind them, and right in his eyes. It was a bad mistake. He should have gone the other way down the back of the buildings and come out further east. That way it would have been them, not he, who was squinting and seeing dark faces devoid of any features. Now he understood something both his father and Marshal Horn had told him – that there's no substitute for experience. And providing he didn't die here in this cold street with the sun in his eyes he would never make the same mistake again.

He saw Hap take a step sideways. For a moment it had almost looked as if Campbell James had made a grab for Hap, maybe to use him as a shield. Whether he'd been thwarted by Hap's quick sideways step or whether Campbell had taken in the blood-soaked figure in front of him and figured he didn't need a shield Casey didn't know. What he did know was that John Stark smiled. Despite the sun being behind Stark, Casey could still see the man grinning. Campbell James, too.

'I don't know what you're talking about,' Stark said.

'We had nothing to do with your daddy's dying,' James said.

'So you're liars as well as cowardly killers,' Casey said. He started to edge closer to the two men, shuffling forward, each step raising a stablike pain in his left shoulder.

'You'd better stop still, Casey,' Stark said. 'You come any closer and we may have to stop you.'

Casey stopped. He was close enough anyway. His Colt still hung in his right hand. Both Stark and James held rifles. So long as he was accurate there'd be no contest.

'The marshal's coming, Casey,' Hap said. Casey could see the undertaker as a shape in his peripheral vision, but he didn't take his eyes off Stark and James. Around him he could hear people talking and running, even hear their whispers reaching out to him over the cold ground, but he took no notice of any of it. He knew somewhere that Hudson had hold of Sam. Though even that thought – and all that came with it – had to be put aside for the moment.

'I don't need the marshal, Hap,' Casey said.

'Don't do anything silly, Casey.'

'You heard the man,' Campbell James said.

'You killed my father,' Casey said. 'There's nothing silly about exacting revenge.'

'You understand revenge?' John Stark said.

'Yes.'

'Then you understand why somebody – not us – might have killed your father.'

'My father gave every man he ever killed the opportunity to give himself up first. He only shot those who were fool enough not to.' Casey paused, then added: 'I'll even extend the same consideration to you.'

'And what about those who gave themselves up and

141

then went to the gallows?' This was Hudson Ranier, coming out of the shadows by Sloppy's, one arm locked around Sam's neck, the other holding a pistol. The barrel of the pistol was pointing to her head. 'He as good as murdered those men.'

Casey looked across the street at Hudson. Hudson was fifteen yards or more away from Stark and James. It meant Casey couldn't keep his eyes on all three of them simultaneously. Whether they'd planned it this way or whether it was just luck he didn't know. He suspected the latter. Sam's face was red. There was blood on her cheek and fear in her eyes. She looked as though she was struggling to breathe.

'Let her go, Hudson. She's your own sister, for goodness' sake.'

'She's no good,' Hudson said. 'No good at all. But I won't hurt her. Leastways not if—'

'Stop that, James!' Casey said and flicked his eyes back towards Campbell. The red-haired man had been slowly raising his rifle whilst Casey's attention had been on Hudson. Now Casey raised his revolver. 'I think you'd best drop those guns, boys.'

'No need to drop 'em, boys,' Hudson said, clicking the hammer back on his gun. 'Ol' Yellow's just about to drop his gun. Ain't you, Yellow?'

Casey caught Sam's eyes. She was at more of an angle to him than Campbell James and John Stark were and the sun made less of a silhouette of her face. She looked terrified but he was sure she shook her head. Now he looked back at Stark and James. They were grinning wider than ever. Hudson raised the barrel of his pistol and rested it gently against Sam's temple.

'Your gun, Yellow,' he said.

'Do it,' Hap whispered.

Casey looked from Hudson to Stark to James and back

142

again. He felt the weight of a fifty pairs of eyes on him from the plank-walks and windows of Main Street. He heard someone running, heavy footsteps on the wood, someone breathing hard. He didn't have to look. He knew it was Marshal Horn.

'You killed my father,' he said to Hudson. 'You all killed him. Your friend told me about it. I have witnesses too.'

'Boys,' Horn said, from behind Casey, and with the words came the sound of a rifle action being snapped. 'I think you *all* should put down your guns.'

'Can't do that, Marshal,' Hudson said. 'Young Casey here's accusing us of killing his father. We don't take kindly to that sort of talk. Specially from no yellow-bellied stranger.'

'I'm not a stranger,' Casey said.

'I told you to leave town,' Marshal Horn said. He was standing level with Casey now.

'Unfinished business,' Casey said. He looked swiftly to the left as he spoke. The marshal looked scared. His face was white and his eyes tired. This was too much for him, four men with guns, a girl being held hostage, and already one dead cowboy on the ground. When Casey looked back he saw Stark now had his rifle raised. For a second Casey found it hard to focus. The sun was in his eyes and everything wavered momentarily. He could still feel the blood running down his flank. He didn't know much about such things but he did know that you couldn't keep bleeding and stay standing up and alert.

'You put your gun down,' Horn said to him. 'We can then sort this out.'

'Tell them to put their guns down.'

'You first,' Horn said.

'Why me?'

'Like the man said – you're the stranger round these parts. There was no trouble till you arrived.'

'Someone killing my father in cold blood was no trouble?'

'He shouldn't have come back.' That was Campbell James.

'He was tricked into coming back,' Casey said.

'He got exactly what he deserved,' Hudson said. He was smiling widely now. All the cards, it seemed, were falling right for him.

'What about Suzie Cobb?' Casey said, throwing another quick glance to his left. 'You want to know who killed her?'

'We figured it was you,' Campbell James said.

'Milton killed her,' Casey said, and the whispers from the plank-walk rose slightly in volume. 'He killed her because he couldn't keep his mouth shut about killing my father. He had to tell someone – to boast about being a killer. So he told Suzie. And when Milton found out that she'd told me he killed her.'

'You have no proof,' Horn said.

'I don't need proof. I know.'

'And who killed Milton?' Horn asked.

'I did,' John Stark said.

'You might want to come down to my office,' Horn said.

'Milton was just about to cut her face off with his knife,' Hudson said. 'John Stark saved her.' As if realizing that such a statement sounded strange coming from a man who was currently holding the girl in question around the neck with a gun to her head he released her. It wasn't as if he could shoot her anyway, not with the marshal there now. Sam fell to the floor gasping for air.

'If that's the case,' Horn said, 'then it shouldn't be too much trouble. Now, you boys *all* drop your guns.'

Casey looked from Hudson to John Stark to Campbell James, then to Hap, and last of all to Sam, kneeling there on the floor, tears and blood on her face.

And he crouched down and laid his Colt .45 on the ground.

*

'No,' Sam said. It didn't seem right. After all that Casey had been through, not just losing his father, but being accused of murder, being kidnapped and almost being murdered himself. It wasn't right that his vow to seek revenge should end here on Main Street with everyone looking on. Hudson was grinning. Campbell James and John Stark too. Only Hap Smith looked relieved. Maybe somewhere deep inside he'd feared he'd be measuring up another Angelo before the morning was through. This way, despite the humiliation, at least Casey was alive. But that was Hap, not her. Even as Hudson had her by the throat, his whiskey breath and his thick arm choking her and the barrel of his gun wavering by her temple, she had been willing Casey to shoot. She had faith in him, faith in God too, and that God would give him a straight shot. And now she couldn't believe he was slumping down, admitting defeat. But look at him – so much blood. It was a wonder he had stood up so long. Maybe it had been too much to ask of such a young man, especially after the last few days.

'Yes,' Hudson said. 'Ol' Yellow's finally realized his limitations.'

Now Marshal Horn lowered his rifle, stepped across in front of Casey and picked up the Colt. He stuck into his waistband.

'You can have this back once you're on the next train, son.' Then he turned to Hudson and his men. 'You boys, too. Guns down. One killing's enough for any morning.' There seemed to be a swagger about the marshal now. Sam noticed the colour coming back into his face as if a bad pain in his head was clearing.

'Can't do that, Marshal,' Hudson said. 'The boy said some things about us and we can't just let them go.'

'Put your gun down, Hud,' Sam said, looking up at him. 'Can't you see it's over?' Casey was slumped down, not quite on his knees, but crouched down on his haunches like an Indian smoking a peace pipe. His head was bowed and his hands were wrapped around his waist as if his whole body was racked with pain. She could see blood dripping on to the floor beneath him. She wanted to go to him, to hold him. She was terrified that he might be dying. They could at least get him to the doc. But no one was moving yet. The shadows and windows were still full of whispers and eyes but no one was daring to come out into the street.

'It's not over,' Hudson said.

The colour that had briefly returned to the marshal's face started to fade again. Sam could smell the whiskey on Hudson's breath even from down on the floor. He wasn't renowned for good judgement whilst sober, let alone drunk.

'Don't be silly, Hud,' she said.

'Boys,' Hudson said. His eyes were unblinking now, staring at the crouched figure of Casey.

'You put your guns down,' Horn said. 'Casey's put his down. We need to get him to the doctor.'

'You step aside, Marshal,' Hudson said.

Sam saw both John Stark and Campbell James glance at Hudson. He nodded and now Campbell James raised his gun too.

'I'm warning you,' Horn said. 'I don't want no more killing here.'

'Step aside, Marshal,' Hudson said.

Now Sam stood up.

'No!' she cried and tried to grab Hudson's gun hand. He flicked the gun sideways and the barrel caught her on the forehead. It hadn't seemed like a hard blow but her knees suddenly buckled and she was back on the floor.

Somebody gasped loudly from the plank-walk behind her and she heard Hap saying that they ought to listen to the marshal.

Then she saw the marshal trying to raise his rifle but getting the barrel caught on Casey's gun which he had stuffed into his waistband just moments before.

Casey knew it was coming, but not precisely when. He held his hands tight around his waist as if he was in pain, but his right hand grasped his father's gun which he'd slid into the back of his belt in Hap's kitchen. He kept his head bowed but his eyes open. Things had gone too far. He'd pushed them and pushed them. He'd escaped from them and he'd driven one of their own – the one that now lay dead – to the point of confession. He'd even turned Hudson's sister against her own kin. Or at least that's the way Hudson would see it. So he knew it was coming. He also figured that maybe the marshal would draw some fire. He knew the old man was out of his depth and he wanted to warn him, to push him aside, but Horn would have been too proud. He knew that. Just as he knew that he didn't have the strength for a prolonged fight. So he thought back to his father lying frozen in that coffin outside Hap's and he thought of how it had felt to slip off that horse into a solitary darkness where he truly believed he was going to die, and he thought of his mother weeping back in Omaha and he thought of how Hudson had held that gun to Sam's head and had even pistol whipped her to her knees when she tried to struggle with him. He thought of all of this and he prayed for forgiveness for not pushing Horn out of the way. And then he saw Hudson nod to his two men.

Casey started to rise, his hand pulling his father's gun from his pants. For a moment he didn't think he'd be quick enough. He saw Stark's finger tightening on the trigger, then his own gun was level, and he was aiming instinctively and squeezing the trigger. The two explosions seemed to be simultaneous but Casey saw the impact of his bullet knocking Stark backwards just as the man fired. He guessed neither Stark nor Campbell had expected him to rise so quickly and probably neither of them had considered that he might have had a second gun. They hadn't been ready for him. Neither of them had even been looking at him as he had exploded upwards, using the last of his strength. To his left he heard the marshal fall to the floor with a grunt and a curse. Campbell James turned his shocked eyes towards Casey. Stark was already stumbling backwards under the force of Casey's bullet. The shot had hit Stark in the chest. Blood fountained out from between his shoulder-blades and his eyes widened in surprise even as the strength in his body evaporated and he fell backwards. Casey would have liked to have said something to Stark. Stark seemed to have been different from the others. Another time, another place, Casey had even thought that they might have been friends. Except for the fact that Stark had murdered his father. And where friendship might have flourished, given different circumstances, revenge was now served. But there was no time to savour this moment. Any pleasure would come later, if at all. Already Casey was turning his gun on to Campbell James and seeing the panic in his eyes. James loosed off a shot that went wild. Casey didn't miss. His father had taught him well.

'Doesn't matter how fast you are, Casey,' he'd said. 'If you're not accurate you might as well be the slowest man there. You're certain to be the deadest.' Despite these words Casey wasn't slow and his bullet tore into James's throat. He was, Casey suspected, dead before he even hit the ground. As the echoes of the shots started to bounce back from the distant mountains and the screams of the townsfolk started to pierce the dullness that the gunshots had created in his ears Casey turned towards Hudson. Despite it being John Stark who had physically fired the shots that had killed his father it was Hudson whom he considered the real killer. Hudson had masterminded the plot to bring his father back to Tyburn Ridge. Hudson had organized his band of men in the best way possible to ambush and kill Robert Angelo.

Hudson was scrambling on the floor, pulling Sam back up to her feet, hiding behind her, a look of shock and fear on his white face.

'I'll kill her!' Hudson said. 'I will.'

'You'll die,' Casey said.

Hudson's gun hand was shaking but he held the barrel close to Sam's head. She was struggling to get away. But fear had given Hudson strength and now he had one arm bent behind her back so hard that she was grimacing in pain and having to stand on tiptoe.

'This is murder!' Hudson was saying. It almost looked as if he might burst into tears. 'You saw it, Marshal.'

Behind him Casey could hear the marshal still cursing and groaning, but struggling to his feet.

Casey raised his gun. 'It was self defence, Hudson. You know it.'

'You shot my boys.'

Casey held his revolver ready. 'You got a choice,' he said. 'You drop the gun and let Sam go and I'll let the marshal take it from here.'

'You'll shoot me.'

'I will if you don't let her go.'

'I ain't done nothing wrong.'

'Then you've got nothing to worry about.'

'Marshal, take his gun off him.'

Marshal Horn stood next to Casey. There was blood staining the left hand side of his coat but he stood tall and erect.

'I'd say your boys were aiming at me right then, Hudson.'

Hudson started to pull Sam back towards the plank-walk on that side of the street. Both Casey and Horn walked in pace with him.

'How would I know who they were aiming at?' he said.

'You have anything to do with the killing of Robert Angelo?' the marshal asked.

'No!'

'Then let Samantha go.'

Hudson's eyes flicked from Casey to the marshal.

'You'll set me up.'

'You'll get a fair trial.'

The torment inside Hudson's mind was etched on his face. Casey could see him fighting with his own fears and emotions and terrors.

'You've got a count of three,' Casey said.

'Marshal, this isn't fair.'

'One.'

The marshal stared at him stony-eyed.

'Two.'

'I'll kill her!'

'Let her go, Hudson. For your own sake.'

'Three.'

Hudson burst into action. He pushed Sam away and simultaneously dropped into a crouch, raising his pistol, the barrel wavering between Casey and the marshal. Hudson squeezed the trigger. The gun wasn't steady enough. The man was in too much torment to have any hope of aiming straight.

Casey aimed and fired even as Hudson sent his bullet high over the marshal's head. That had been Hudson's only chance. Casey's shot caught him in the bicep of his gun arm. He grunted in pain and the gun spun from his grip. Now he bent over in pain, clutching at his wound, looking up at Casey with eyes like a frightened animal.

As the marshal walked towards him Hudson started to scrabble towards his gun. Casey fired again and Hudson's gun spun three yards down the street.

'It's over, Hudson,' Casey said. And with the words came a light-headedness and a faintness that swept over him like a dust storm. The last thing he saw before he blacked out was the marshal leaning over Hudson, his gun drawn, and his face hard as rock.

CHAPTER TWELVE

Every movement of the train sent a twinge through Casey's shoulder and into his neck. Occasionally there was a heavier than normal jolt as the train crossed junctions and the twinge became more of a stabbing pain. He closed his eyes and rested his head against the back of the seat. It was hard to get comfortable but he was so tired that even the discomfort and the pain slowly faded into the background as sleep mercifully stole up on him. Soon he was barely aware of his surroundings, there was just the distant sound of a lady talking to a child, the clickity-clack of the carriage wheels upon the track, and an occasional whistle from the locomotive. It had been cold when he climbed aboard that morning, the temperature eating into his wound and making it more lively, but as they headed east the carriage began to warm up, and now even the temperature was sleep-inducing.

The previous afternoon he'd woken up in Hap's. He was lying in Hap's bed and the undertaker was sitting alongside him. It felt like a horse had kicked him in the shoulder.

'You're awake,' Hap said, and smiled. He was dressed in his usual black.

'I bet not many of your patients wake up,' Casey said.

'It would shock me if they did.'

Casey managed a smile and Hap called out to someone

that he was awake. A moment later Sam burst into the room. She was smiling and looking prettier than Casey had ever seen her. Maybe it was the way the afternoon sun seeped into the room, he thought, but even as the thought crossed his mind he realized it was sheer delight that was lighting up her face that way.

'You're awake!'

'Indeed I am. You look mighty pretty,' he said. 'I'd have tried to wake up sooner had I known.'

'Oh shush,' she said.

'Are you OK?' The events of the morning were slowly untangling themselves in his fogged mind and he could recall blood running down her face from where Milton had cut her, and he could recall Hudson almost choking her.

'I'm fine.'

'He cut you?'

'Milton?'

'Yes.'

'It was just a tiny cut. You can't see it unless you look close. Anyway, I've put some powder on.'

'I'm sorry about all that.'

'Shush.'

'What time is it?'

'It's two o'clock,' Hap said. 'You've been asleep for more than four hours.'

'You were exhausted,' Sam said.

'And you've lost a lot of blood. We were…'

'You were what, Hap?'

'We were worried for a while.'

'I'm OK.'

'I've got some broth on the stove,' Sam said. 'Do you want some right now?'

Casey stretched and grimaced in pain.

'Tell me what happened first,' he said.

*

Hudson was in the jailhouse and Milton, Campbell James, and John Stark were in coffins. Marshal Horn had left instruction that the moment Casey woke up he was to be called. He'd been in twice already – once at midday and once at 1.30 to check on Casey. After they'd brought him up to speed and fed him a bowl of broth, Hap said maybe he ought to go and find Horn. After he'd gone Casey looked across at Sam. It seemed to him that a sadness was creeping into her eyes.

'Are you all right?' he asked.

She nodded.

'It's a lot to take in, isn't it,' he said.

'Everything's changed.'

'That's all it takes. A couple of bullets.'

'I don't mean this morning. I mean, the whole thing. My brother setting up your father that way.'

Now it was Casey's turn to nod.

'He put so much thought into it,' Sam said. 'He's never put that much thought into anything.'

'It must have been burning him up from the inside out. The need to get even.'

'I want to hate him.'

'But he's your brother.'

'Did you mean to shoot him like that? Just in the arm, I mean.'

'Yes.'

'You'd have been within your rights to have killed him.'

'Believe me, part of me wanted to.'

'But?'

'But nothing.'

'If it hadn't been for me, would you have killed him?'

The way she was looking at him it felt as if her eyes could see right into his head. He was scared to lie.

'I might have done,' he said. 'Though I don't like to kill anyone if I don't have to.'

'But you came here for vengeance.'

He nodded. 'And to take my father home.'

They looked at each other again. There was so much unsaid, so much neither of them seemed brave enough to say.

'Are you going to be all right?' she said, fumbling for words with which to break the silence.

'It's just a flesh wound.'

'When are you going home?'

And there it was. The words he didn't want to hear. The way she said it he knew that this was where it ended. In fact, somewhere deep inside he'd known all along that if he did what he'd come to do then the repercussions would almost certainly mean she'd feel differently about him. He longed to tell her that he wanted her to accompany him back to Omaha, to tell her of what a beautiful home he had there, that *they* could have there. He wanted her to step a little closer. He wanted to kiss her. To tell her that . . .

'He's going home tomorrow,' Marshal Horn said, swinging the door open and walking in, cold air coming off his coat. His voice was as stern as it had been when he had been questioning Casey about Suzie Cobb's death but his lips were curled up in a slight smile. 'Glad you're back in the land of the living, son.'

'Thank you, Marshal.'

'How you feeling?'

'Fine.'

The marshal laughed. 'Seems to me you wouldn't say otherwise no matter how you felt.'

'And how about you?' The marshal had a different coat on. He'd lost some blood too, yet he'd not slumped into unconsciousness the way Casey had.

'Oh I'm fine, thank you. The bullet was in and out quicker than a . . .' He glanced at Samantha and refrained from saying what he was going to say. 'I've been shot worse than that before. It was a surprise more than anything.'

'There looked like a lot of blood from what I remember.'

'You get to my age, son, you'll find out you can manage on a whole lot less blood.'

'You're a good lawman, Marshal Horn.'

'I'm a little slow, is all.'

'Speed isn't what matters.'

'I think it is. You were darn quick out there.'

'I wasn't quick enough. If those boys could have kept their heads and shot straight then maybe neither of us would be here.'

'But they didn't. Not many folks can.'

'Nevertheless, I didn't play it right. I shouldn't have put you in that position.'

'You did fine, Casey,' Hap said.

'You sure did.'

'I am sorry for all the trouble,' Casey said.

'Stop apologizing, son. It was coming anyway. If I'd have put you on the train two days ago it might have postponed it. That's all. These things build up and build up. Something would have triggered those boys sooner or later. Probably sooner.'

'What's going to happen to him?'

'Hudson?'

'Yeah.'

Horn never answered for a moment. He glanced across at Sam then back at Casey.

'He tried to kill us, Casey. He threatened to kill Samantha. His own sister. He was instrumental in killing your father. Hap told me about the note. He told me about how they tried to hang you, too.'

156

'So what's going to happen to him?'
'I imagine he'll hang.'

After Horn had left Casey wanted to recapture the moment
that had existed fleetingly before he had come in. But now
the atmosphere had changed. He hadn't killed her brother
but he might as well have done. Hudson would hang. It felt
as much Casey's fault as anyone's. Now he realized why they
had left town all those years before. His father had once
loved Violet Ranier and he had sent her husband to the
gallows. It had been too much for his father to bear. Oh, it
had had to be done. It was his father's job. But he'd never
be able to face her again. So they packed up and left. And
his father had never told anyone. He'd kept it all to
himself. Even Casey's mother had never asked. At least, if
she did Casey wasn't there when that conversation took
place. And now, ten years later, Casey understood.

'Sam,' he said.

She shook her head. There were tears in her eyes.

'It's OK, Casey.'

'No it's not.'

'It wasn't your doing.'

'Sam.'

'Don't.'

'I want to ask you something.'

'Please don't.'

'I have to.'

'No.

'When I go back—'

'Please don't ask, Casey.'

'Why?'

'I've got to go now. I'm sorry.'

And with that she swept out of the room, the door
swinging closed behind her, but not so fast that he didn't
hear the first of her sobs.

*

She wasn't there on the station platform. Hap was there, dressed all in black with his glasses on. In fact Hap had given him a ride from town to the station in his buggy with Robert Angelo's coffin in the back. Later, Hap said, he was going to bury Milton, Campbell, and John Stark.

'It's too many coffins to be carrying around in one day. But especially this one.'

'I appreciate all you've done, Hap.'

'You're a good boy, Casey.'

Casey nodded. 'I just try to do what's right, Hap. Sometimes it's not easy.'

They rode in silence for a while. Ahead of them they could see the train already at the platform, the engine being refilled with water from the tower at the east end of the station. Casey glanced over his shoulder. He had been doing so for the entire ride.

'Maybe she'll be at the station,' Hap said.

'My father killed her father,' Casey said. 'I as good as hung her brother.'

'You never know,' Hap said, and smiled thinly.

'Those are hard things to forgive, Hap.'

'You didn't do anything wrong.'

'Maybe not. But it feels like it.'

Marshal Horn was already on the platform.

'It seems like you've been here for ever, Casey,' he said.

'It feels that way to me too.'

'I'm sorry you got hurt. I'm sorry any of this happened at all.'

'You were the one who told me to stop apologizing yesterday, Marshal.'

'I know. You're right.' He held out his hand. 'Come back and see us sometime.'

Hap found a guard and together with Casey and Horn

they loaded Robert Angelo's coffin on to the last car of the train.

'I guess this is it,' Casey said.

'I guess so.'

'Godspeed,' Hap said.

And Casey climbed aboard the eastbound Union Pacific, heading for Omaha and home.

She sat down beside him, careful not to wake him. He shouldn't have been travelling so soon, not with all the blood he'd lost. But he was anxious to get his father home. Hap thought it was wise also. Even in winter you didn't want to leave a man unburied for too long.

Deep down she'd known all along that she wanted to be with him. It was too real, too close to what she'd dreamed of to let slip away. He'd been about to ask her yesterday and it had broken her heart to rush out and leave him with that devastated look in his eyes. But her mind had been a whirlpool of conflicting emotions and she hadn't been able to face even having to think about the decision. Not that running away had helped. She'd lain awake all night. But though she had tortured herself with the question of whether to go or stay she had known all along that she would go. She had fallen in love with him. And he with her. Of that she was sure. It had been almost impossibly hard to leave her mother and even her brother.

'I'm only a railroad ride away,' she'd told herself and her mother that morning and had ridden into town with nothing but the clothes on her back. Nez Sully would look after her horse and she'd return soon to gather her few belongings and to say her goodbyes properly.

At first she'd been scared to show her face. Casey and Hap and Horn had been loading the coffin into the train when she'd slipped on board.

And here she was now, looking down at the long lashes

resting on his face, the stubble around his jaw, the lines creasing the edges of his eyes as if such a young man had already seen too much. And maybe he had. His skin still looked pale from the blood he'd lost and every now and then he murmured as if in pain, or at least a little discomfort. She watched him for a long time and eventually, unable to bear it any longer she reached out and gently took his hand in hers. He stirred, but didn't wake.

That was OK. When he did, she'd be there.